THE BILLIONAIRE HUSBAND TEST

BILLIONAIRE ONLINE DATING SERVICE BOOK #1

ELLE JAMES

TWISTED PAGE INC

THE BILLIONAIRE HUSBAND TEST

BILLIONAIRE ONLINE DATING SERVICE BOOK #1

New York Times & *USA Today*
Bestselling Author

ELLE JAMES

Ebook ISBN: 978-1-62695-011-5

Print ISBN: 978-1-62695-016-0

To all my lovely readers out there, may you find love. Whether it be online, with family, in a story or with your favorite pooch or kitty. Hugs from me to you!

Elle James

CHAPTER 1

"DON'T LEAVE love up to luck. With the help of my firm and heavily tested computer algorithms, you will have a ninety-nine point nine percent chance of finding your perfect match." The attractive young woman, wearing a soft gray business suit and standing in front of the white board, clicked a hand-held remote control. A picture of a couple embracing at sunset on a beach materialized on the white surface. "What do you think? Willing to give my program a shot?"

"I don't know." Frank Cooper Johnson sat at the conference table with the other members of the Billionaires Anonymous Club. "Am I the only one who thinks this is a bad idea?"

"Mr. Johnson—" Leslie Lamb began.

"Call him Coop. All his friends call him that." Maxwell Smithson grinned.

"For the sake of argument, give my friend Leslie the benefit of the doubt." Taggert Bronson rose to stand beside the presenter. "Think about it. Didn't we all make the same plans? Work hard, work smart, make our first million by thirty, start a family by thirty-five...We're all on track—only better–instead of millions, we made our billions by thirty." Tag pointed to Gage Tate. "How's that media empire going?" He nodded toward Sean O'Leary. "Your oil speculating has you sitting pretty, doesn't it, Sean? And Coop, you and I are making billions on our financial investments. Have any of you even thought about the next step in our plan? How many of you are even dating?"

Sean raised his hand. "I've been dating."

"The same girl more than once?" Tag asked.

"Using a computer to find a mate just doesn't seem right." Coop pushed back his chair and rose. "When I find the woman I want to marry, I'll do it the old-fashioned way."

Tag snorted. "And meet her at a bar?"

"Any of you have any luck lately going to a bar and not being slammed by the paparazzi?"

Gage sighed. "Though I hate to admit it, the man has a point. I can't step outside my condo without being hit by at least a dozen cameras, much less go to dinner with anyone without being bombarded."

Leslie smiled. "That's the beauty of BODS—"

"Seriously?" Sean shook his head. "BODS?"

The woman drew herself up to her full five-foot-three inches and stared down her nose at Sean. "Billionaire Online Dating Service—BODS. It's an acronym, so sue me. As I was saying, the beauty of the system is that the communication is all done anonymously. You meet real woman, not money-grubbing, limelight-seeking gold-diggers."

Gage frowned. "They won't know that we're loaded?"

"Financial status is not one of the questions we ask on the online data collection system. I perform a background check on each entrant and the computer does the matching."

Tag spread his hands. "Don't you love it? And the match is all based on your own personality profile." He dropped his hands when none of the others spoke. "What have you got to lose?"

Shaking his head, Coop grumbled, "Our dignity. Participation is admitting we're hopeless at finding a date."

Leslie shook her head. "Not at all. The program gives you a better chance of finding someone who truly fits the life-style of your dreams. Tell you what. As my first customers—"

Gage shot to his feet. "Whoa, wait a minute. First?" He stared across at Tag. "I thought you said this system was proven?"

"It is...on volunteers." Tag held up his hands. "Leslie hasn't yet charged for her services. Calm down."

Coop crossed his arms, ready for the meeting to be over. "I don't relish being someone's guinea pig."

"You aren't." Leslie sucked in a deep breath and let it out. "Tell you what, how about I let you use my service free? If you find the woman of your dreams, then you pay me what you think the experience was worth."

"Can't get fairer than that." Tag grinned. "Who wants to be first to sign up?"

"I think you should be." Cooper pinned Tag with a challenging stare.

"I'm already in the system and aiming for a date next Friday." Tag's eyes narrowed. "How about it, Coop? Or are you afraid?"

Hell yeah, Cooper was afraid. What kind of loser would the computer match him up with? Then again, he wouldn't admit to any of them that the idea of dating was worse than public speaking...and he hated public speaking. That's why he worked the financial market and stayed behind the scenes. He lived on his ranch, raised his horses quietly—no fanfare and no paparazzi as long as he didn't step out on a date. So far, the arrangement had been very lucrative with no distractions. Lonely, but lucrative, about summed up his life.

"Look, Leslie is in a situation no different than we

were when we started out." Tag continued, "Give her business a chance. One date. That's all she's asking."

"Fine," Cooper said. "Anything to get this meeting over with."

Leslie's face bloomed with a huge smile. "I'll take you in Tag's office, one at a time to enter your data and show you the ropes. The process won't take long and you'll have your match. You won't regret your decision. I promise."

Cooper was already regretting his agreement, and he hadn't even been matched yet.

EMMA JACOB'S cell phone vibrated, indicating a text message. Sitting at a stoplight, she glanced at the message and sighed.

Set an extra plate at dinner. The message was from her oldest brother, Ace. More than likely, the guest was another attempt at fixing her up with a man. For the past month, all four of her brothers had taken it upon themselves to find Emma a husband.

Great, that's all she needed, more husband candidates forced on her by the worst matchmakers ever in Jacobs family history. Granted, her four brothers meant well, but really? If she'd wanted another man in her life, she'd have gone out and chosen one herself.

Truth was she was happy just the way things

were. Well, almost. She'd have been much happier if the love of her life had lived long enough for them to be married, have children and grow old together. But that hadn't been in the cards. Not once Marcus was deployed, got hit by an improvised explosion device and died before being transported back to the states.

Her throat tightened and she twisted the diamond engagement ring on her finger. For two years, she'd been mourning his death. You'd think her brothers would let it be, instead of telling her she should get back in the saddle.

Emma slipped the ring from her finger and tucked it into her wallet. Maybe removing the ring would lead her brothers to think she was ready to move on, even if she wasn't. That and her trip to Dallas and a meeting with the one friend, Leslie Lamb, she'd made in her grieving group would set her plan in motion. Emma had a special favor to ask of her friend. One she hoped would solve all her problems with her brothers.

"You want what?" Leslie leaned across her desk an hour later, tapping her pen against the notepad she'd been scribbling on.

"I want you to set me up on a date with a man that will completely fail to impress my brothers." Emma ticked off on her fingers. "He has to be nice looking. That fact will throw off the boys. Preferably someone who makes his living sitting behind a desk." She'd pictured a pasty computer geek, but didn't want to be that crude in front of Leslie.

"Let me get this straight. You want this date to fail?" Leslie shook her head. "I'm building a business, not tearing it down. How will that look to the guy I'm setting you up with if I match him with someone totally wrong for his preferences?"

Emma sat back, frowning. "Hmm, sorry. That's pretty narrow-minded, thinking only of myself." She chewed on her lip for a moment. "I guess I could go find some other online dating service and play Russian roulette." She sat up. "I'm sorry, Leslie, the idea was stupid. Just forget I asked. I know how hard you've worked to put together the business plan and line up investors for your dating service. I wish you lots of luck." Emma gathered her purse and stood. "I have to get back to the ranch before feeding time."

"Wait." Leslie left her chair and rounded her desk, laying a hand on Emma's arm. "Do me a favor first and fill out a form on my computer. Be honest, don't fudge the data and let's see what happens."

Already shaking her head, Emma backed toward the door. "I don't want to set you up for failure. I'm really not interested in finding love. I had it."

Leslie squeezed her arm. "I know. Thinking of loving anyone else is hard, isn't it? I know exactly where you are. I haven't even tried, yet."

"Yet. At least you might some day." Emma shook

her head, pain pinching her throat. "Not me. I had the love of my life. I don't want second best."

"At least, give the system a chance to find a match that closely suits you. Give him one date, and maybe your brothers will get off your back."

"I don't know. I don't like leading someone on when I don't want it to go anywhere."

"Just do it and keep an open mind. We screen our clients and do background checks. At least, you know you won't be getting an ex-con or child molester. You won't regret it, I promise."

Emma chewed on her lip. Leslie's proposal might do the trick. She just didn't want her friend's matchmaking business to suffer the consequences. "The date is doomed to failure. Are you sure you want to take the hit?"

"Be honest with the data. The system will do the rest and I'm willing to take the risk."

For a long moment, Emma stared into her friend's hopeful face. "Anyone ever tell you saying no to you is hard?" She laughed. "If you keep that up, you should get lots of business."

Leslie nodded, a smug smile on her lips. "I plan on it. I only want others to have a chance at the love you and I have both known. I wouldn't have missed the experience for the world."

Emma sighed. "Me either." She let Leslie lead her into a spare office where she could use the computer to enter her data. Emma made a point of putting it all out there—the good, the bad and the not so attractive. If the system found someone to date her, the result would be a miracle. And once out at the ranch with her brothers running him through his paces, any prospect would soon learn no one would equal their expectations.

She'd be off the hook and free to pursue her own goals and dreams. Which included purchasing Old Man Rausch's one-hundred-and-fifty-acre spread on Willow Creek. The place would be all hers, paid for with the money she'd been saving from her work as a horse trainer for the T-Bar-M Ranch. Once she lived on her own, her brothers couldn't interfere with her life.

A good plan, and one she intended to see through.

As she stepped into her truck to make the long drive back to the Rockin' J Ranch, a cool breeze swept across the parking lot, lifting the hair off the back of her neck, surrounding her like a caress. She glanced at the sky. No clouds. Weird. The temperature read-out on the bank sign on the corner listed ninety-nine degrees. Heat waves rippled upward from the black pavement, and Emma had yet to switch on the truck AC. So where had the cool breeze come from? She could swear she smelled a faint hint of musky aftershave, the kind Marcus liked to wear when they'd gone out on dates.

Emma's chest tightened and she sat still, trying to recapture the scent. Finally, she gave up. She had to be imagining the smell. All this talk with Leslie about having loved the man of their dreams had played havoc with her memories. Nothing a good round of stall mucking wouldn't cure.

She'd never told anyone she thought Marcus's spirit lingered around her, keeping her company when she was lonely or afraid. Her brothers would have her in a shrink's office quicker than she could say *lickety-split*. At night, when she lay in bed, missing him so badly it hurt, a light breeze would stir the curtains and waft around her. She'd stare at the picture of them laughing on the beach at South Padre Island and sigh. Marcus was everything she'd ever wanted in life. With him gone, she didn't have anything to aim for, except the ranch and her independence.

If her plan to bring a "date" home to her brothers worked, she'd be one step closer to that independence she so craved and to quelling her brothers' determination to marry her off. The ball was in Leslie's court to find the right man to pull off the plan.

"Please be everything I asked for," Emma whispered as she cranked the truck engine. Another gentle breeze blew in through the open window and trailed across her skin, lifting more goose bumps. She shrugged and shifted into drive. Emma chastised herself for her morbid thoughts. If she didn't stop thinking every peculiar thing that happened in her life was a sign, she'd be forced to commit herself to the nearest psychiatric ward for evaluation.

CHAPTER 2

"L<small>ET US KNOW HOW IT GOES</small>," Tag insisted. "Since you're the first bull out of the chute, we're counting on you to make us proud." Cooper's friend chuckled into the phone. "I can practically hear the wedding bells already."

Cooper juggled the phone and switched on his blinker, pulling off the highway where the directions indicated. "Tag, get real. I'm not going to marry the woman after one date. I'm giving this friend of yours one shot at this online dating thing and that's all. I don't want to hear any more after today. Got that?"

"Sure, sure. I get it." Tag paused. "Still, let us know."

Cooper didn't bother responding, instead he clicked the end button and stared up at the sign arching over the gate.

Rockin' J Ranch.

His stomach roiled. Why couldn't this woman meet him in Dallas for dinner, like normal people? Having him out to the ranch on the first date was...well...different. Not that he minded, preferring the outdoors to the city streets any day of the week. And this arrangement would preclude any chance of the press getting wind of this billionaire and his date.

The woman Leslie had set him up with had gone so far as to leave specific instructions, telling him to wear jeans and boots. He didn't like the sound of the arrangement and wondered if she just wanted a hired hand for the day and couldn't afford the wages. But then how would she have afforded the exorbitant fee Leslie Lamb charged for her company's match-making services?

Nothing about this "date" smelled right. The devil on his shoulder asked him why the hell he'd come, then?

Maybe his agreement had something to do with the picture Leslie had shown him. The woman had smiled at him with clear green eyes, sun-kissed skin and freckles. He'd always been a sucker for a girl with freckles. No model, socialite or city girl this. With her long, straight, sandy-blond hair, she looked like the girl-next-door.

Exactly what he'd pictured himself with for the long haul. Oh, he'd dated the occasional society women, finding very little to talk about besides who was doing who and the latest divorce scandal. With

Emma Jacobs, that was her name, he imagined conversations would be so far away from Dallas's social scene as to be refreshing.

And her answers didn't sound cooked up. She didn't mince words on her responses to her favorite sports, hobbies and foods. She liked horses, rode four-wheelers, hunted, hiked and loved watching football games. Nothing in there hinted to a fetish for buying shoes or designer handbags.

Despite his better judgment on the whole match-making thing, he'd agreed to go on the first date. If nothing else, doing so would get Tag and the rest of the BAs off his back. Then he could go back to his regular life of billionaire recluse, content to hole up on his ranch southwest of Dallas.

He punched the button for the speaker at the gate.

"Yup," a man's deep voice answered.

"Cooper Johnson to see Ms. Emma Jacobs." He shook his head. The formality of the speaker system seemed out of place with the whole Texas ranch thing, but if the machine made them feel safer, so be it.

"Hold on...Hey, Ace," the voice yelled. "It's him. Emma's date!"

Coop groaned inwardly.

"Well, let him in," another voice called out faintly.

"Oh, yeah. Got it." A pause and clicking noises. "Must have left the speaker on. Damned system. I'll never get used to it. Come on in, Cooper. Emma's getting her clothes on."

Cooper shifted into drive, a chuckle rising up his throat. If this was any indication of what his day would be like, he was in for hell. The man on the speaker sounded like a redneck with the IQ of a mule.

The driveway wound through a stand of gnarled red oaks, shading the pavement all the way, without giving Cooper a glimpse of the house until the trees parted at the base of a rise. On top was a large old colonial mansion that would give the plantation houses of the south a run for their money. Surrounded by double decking and creamy-white limestone, the building looked like something straight out of a Texas history book.

And on the porch, three men leaned against the support beams and railing—all large, broad-shouldered and wearing cowboy hats. The welcoming committee, no doubt.

Cooper fought the urge to turn his truck around and drive straight back down the driveway. No woman was worth running a gauntlet of cowboys, even if she looked like the girl-next-door.

Before he could change his mind, he pulled up in the drive and shifted into park.

A truck rounded the corner of the house, dragging a gooseneck trailer, and a fourth cowboy parked and got out. This one looked much like the others.

So the woman had family, or were these her bodyguards?

As Cooper climbed down from the driver's seat, the men on the porch closed in and surrounded his truck, inspecting it like a prize horse.

"The man drives a truck. A four-wheel drive, at that. Can't be all bad." The first man to him stuck out his hand. "Ace Jacobs. Emma's oldest brother."

The man's grip was strong, stronger than necessary. Cooper reckoned the cowboy was testing him. "Cooper Johnson. Nice to meet you." No stranger to a good workout, Cooper squeezed back until his knuckles hurt, keeping a poker face the entire time. Even when he wanted to jerk his hand free and coax the blood back into it.

One by one, each of the four men subjected him to a vice-like handshake. By the time he'd made the rounds, he had a sore hand and four names to remember. Ace, Brand, Colton and Dillon. All Emma's brothers and all interested in sizing him up.

"Emma should be out in a minute," Ace said. "She just got out of the shower."

"And a good thing," said the one who'd identified himself as Colton. "She smelled like a horse."

Nice image. Cooper was wishing he'd turned tail and escaped while he had a chance. Too late. Now, he had to suffer the brother inquisition.

"What do you do for a living, Mr. Johnson?"

"I'm heavy into the stock market," Cooper hedged,

reluctant to say too much. He didn't like telling people he made a pile of money at what he did. The fact changed how they treated him. Mostly, in a bad way.

The one he remembered as Colton crossed both arms over his chest. "So, you don't make an honest living. Instead, you gamble other people's money?"

Cooper shook his head. "I only work with my own money. Keeps it simple."

"Desk jockey, huh?" Ace smirked. "Do much ranchin' with that truck?"

Cooper shrugged. "Some." His truck had hauled its share of trailers loaded with hay and loads of firewood and fence posts. He made sure it got a good cleaning after each, taking pride in the vehicle he'd always dreamed of owning when he was too poor to pay the rent on a ratty apartment.

Dillon leaned against Cooper's truck, arms crossed. "We're hauling hay today. Could use an extra pair of hands if you're willing and able."

"You guys leave the poor man alone," a sultry, husky voice called out. "He's not here to be your hired hand. We have a date."

Cooper turned toward the house. A tall, slender woman stood on the porch with her hands fisted on her hips, a smile tugging at her pale pink lips. She wore a blue chambray shirt five sizes too big, hanging open, the sleeves rolled up to her elbows, a white tank top beneath and jeans so worn they were almost as white as the top. Well-worn, cowboy boots graced her feet. She carried a straw cowboy hat and her hair was braided into one long, thick plait hanging down her back. Her smile broadened as she descended the steps. "I'm Emma. Sorry to keep you waiting."

For a long moment, his gaze followed her every move, his voice lost in the natural sway of her hips and the confidence with which she strode toward him. No woman in a sequined ball gown ever captured his attention and imagination like this cowgirl, all spit and vinegar and no-nonsense attitude, packaged in a long, cool, sexy drink of water.

When she reached out to shake his hand, he gripped hers, feeling the strength and grace all wrapped up in her long fingers. A spark of something ripped through his body.

Her eyes widened. For a moment, she stared, then her lids lowered briefly, hiding the pale green irises. "You can let go of my hand now," she said, her voice low and gravelly.

Cooper could imagine her using that voice beside him in bed. As soon as the thought entered his mind, his cheeks burned and he jerked his hand and his head back into the situation. One man surrounded by a family of five, four of which— hell, maybe five— could kick his ass in a bar fight. "Pleasure to meet you, Emma."

A cool, wet nose nudged his palm and Cooper glanced down.

A light blond golden retriever sat at Cooper's feet, tongue lolling, brown eyes staring upward. "Hey, boy." Cooper squatted to his haunches and scratched behind the dog's ears. "What's your name?"

"Damnedest thing I ever saw." The man called Brand shook his head. "That dog usually barks at every stranger that sets his boots on the ground at the Rockin' J." His gaze shifted from the dog to Cooper.

Ace crossed his arms over his chest, his gaze on the dog. "Marcus gave Emma that dog. He's kinda protective of her. Nelson usually doesn't like other men."

"Guess he approves of day trader here," Dillon noted.

Emma frowned. "Nelson, heel."

The golden retriever hesitated, his snout pointed first at Cooper then Emma, then back to Cooper as if apologizing before he trotted over to Emma and sat at her heels.

Cooper grinned and straightened, glad he'd passed the "family pet" hurdle so easily and sure the rest of them wouldn't be as easily won over. He glanced around, ready to break up the awkward welcoming committee."What's the plan?"

"Our housekeeper prepared a picnic for us," she said.

Colton pushed his cowboy hat back on his head and gave Emma a narrowed glance. "We thought you'd be drivin' the truck while we load the hay."

"Your brothers mentioned that it's hay-hauling day." Cooper's gaze slipped past the four men and rested with Emma. "Am I interfering with work that needs to be done?"

"Like we said...we can always use another set of hands. Unless you think the work would be too hard for a man who trades stock for a livin'." Brand stuck a straw between his lips, his brows raised in challenge. "What's it to be?"

"Cut it out, guys." Emma hooked Cooper's arm and led him up the steps to the house, Nelson trailing. "Ignore them, they're only looking out for me. Besides, I'm sure you didn't come all the way out here to go to work in the hay field."

"I don't mind." Cooper's inner stud couldn't back away from Brand's challenge. He wasn't afraid of hard work. He'd hauled hay all summer for six years straight going through high school and college. The work helped him earn money for rent and food. Though he had ranch hands to help him now, he still pitched in and did his share. "Do you usually help?"

"Normally, I do all the driving, and occasionally help with the loading." She shrugged.

Even that movement she made was so natural and sexy.

Cooper's breath caught and his groin tightened. "Who will drive if you don't?"

"I will." Dillon raised his hand.

"The hell you will. We'll take turns." Colton nodded toward Cooper. "Gonna join us?"

"No way. You guys will kill him." Emma's mouth twitched, a smile tugging on the corners.

Just the hint of her smile had Cooper agreeing to something he hadn't intended. "I'll help, if Emma's needed to drive."

"Are you sure?" Emma's gaze ran the length of him, obviously lacking confidence that he could do the work.

His pride smarting, Cooper squared his shoulders. "Absolutely. Being outdoors will feel good since I spend so much time behind a desk." He didn't, really. Trading stock was so much easier with the mobile applications available, and he did more than trade. Cooper spent more time out on his ranch, when he was home. The rest of the time he traveled —researching companies and investing in those that had good people and a product he could stand behind.

He hadn't hauled hay in a while, but he worked out daily and rode horses as often as possible. How hard would it be to get back into the swing of tossing bales onto a trailer? And working would delay him from being alone with Emma and having to come up with something to say to fill those awkward silences that came with strangers.

FOR THE FIRST HOUR, Emma wanted to laugh at how her brothers put Cooper through his paces. They left him the heaviest bales and cracked crude jokes, perfectly playing the part of obnoxious country rednecks. She hadn't expected Cooper, a man who traded stock for a living, to last four minutes, much less four hours under the wilting heat and back-breaking work. But he'd hung in with the others, working just as hard and long. When he'd pulled off his shirt and Emma almost ran over a hay bale, she realized she might be in trouble. He wasn't at all what she'd wanted Leslie to send.

For a man who made his living behind a desk, he didn't have an ounce of flab and his chest was solid, tanned and positively drool-worthy.

Damn. If he didn't watch it, he'd earn a nod from her brothers and that wasn't the point of this whole exercise. Emma wanted this guy to run scared and for her brothers to rule him out as husband material. By the time they headed back to the barn, the men were all on first-name basis. Cooper laughed and joked right along with her brothers. She had to admit, she admired the man—for sticking it out, and for a lot of other things she'd been working hard for the past three hours to forget—pecks, arms, abs...

Out on the range, Emma wished she'd had reception on her cell phone. She'd have called Leslie and chewed her out for sabotaging her efforts to get her brothers off her back. Instead, she'd sat, stewing in her juices behind the steering wheel as she pulled into the barnyard.

When she climbed out of the truck and faced Cooper, who still had his shirt off, she forced herself to look away. "Thanks," she said.

"Yeah, thanks. We got that done a lot faster with your help." Ace pounded Cooper's back.

"Didn't think a stock trader had it in him, but you proved me wrong." Dillon slapped his cowboy hat against his dusty leg. "You're all right in my books."

Colton nodded. "Yup, you got a keeper there, Emma."

"Don't screw it up." Brand gave Emma a hug.

"Geez, Brand, you stink." Emma pushed him away, realizing she would have to do a lot more to convince her brothers this was the wrong man. She cocked her brows upward and gazed into Cooper's face, trying to act natural, knowing she was about to set him up for the fall. Literally. Hell, desperate times called for desperate measures. "Up for that picnic now?"

Cooper glanced down at his naked chest, gleaming with sweat. "I could do with a shower."

"Got one better than that." Emma went in for the first kill. "I'd planned on taking you to a little pool on

Willow Creek where we could swim and enjoy the lunch Mrs. Fuentez packed."

"That's a great idea." Dillon grinned. "Especially after sweating in the field. Who's in?"

Ace backhanded Dillon in the gut. "I think they'd enjoy it better just the two of them."

Cooper's lips twisted and he scrubbed a hand through his sweaty hair. "I didn't bring a swimsuit."

With an eyebrow arched, Emma smiled. "Swimsuits aren't required." She flounced away, her smile widening. "I'll collect the food." That would get her brothers' dander up. Though she was twenty-five years old, they still treated her like the kid sister who had to be protected and coddled.

Skinny-dipping with a stranger should have all of their brotherly warning bells pinging.

Inside, Emma let the smile fade and she raced for the refrigerator in the kitchen.

Señora Fuentez met her at the door carrying a leather saddle bag, bulging with the picnic items.

"Oh, thank you, Mama Fuentez." Emma pecked the older woman on the cheek.

"What game are you playing *con tus hermanos y el muy apuesto hombre.*"

Emma's cheeks burned and she glanced away from Mrs. Fuentez. "I don't know what you're talking about. I'm not playing any games with my brothers or Cooper."

The housekeeper's eyes narrowed and she hmphed. "You play with fire, *hija*."

"Then I best not get burned, right?" Emma forced a smile, took the saddlebag and turned. "Thank you for the food."

When Emma emerged on the porch, her brothers were smiling and talking with Cooper, teasing him about the pool and clapping him on the back.

"Now, don't do anything I wouldn't do," Colton advised.

"That leaves the field wide open." Ace frowned, digging into his back pocket for his wallet from which he extracted an accordion of condoms. "If you do half of what Colton would do, play it safe." He handed the foil packets to Cooper who accepted them, his cheeks red beneath his tan.

"Seriously?" Emma stomped down the steps. This date was becoming a nightmare. Every step forward in her plan met with several steps backward. "Here." She shoved the saddlebag at Cooper. "Make yourself useful. As for you." She scanned the group and glared at her brothers. "What happened to brotherly over protectiveness?"

"You keep telling us you're twenty-five." Ace crossed his arms. "You can make your own decisions, choose your own path. You don't need us interfering in your love life."

Now, they see the light. Too bad she'd already laid the

groundwork to go skinny-dipping with a veritable stranger. She let her gaze pass over Cooper's naked chest. Not as if she hadn't seen her brother's naked. They swam in front of her unabashed. If she'd seen one man, she shouldn't be at all embarrassed by another.

Then why was her body on fire and her palms sweating? Must be the Texas heat. That had to be it. Her lips firmed. "Let's get this picnic over with."

"Taking the four-wheelers?" Brand asked.

She had planned on taking the ATVs, but given the disaster of Cooper's stellar performance, another idea blossomed in Emma's thoughts. Why her brothers hadn't already thought of it, she didn't know. "I think we'll ride the horses."

"They could use the exercise." Ace nodded toward Cooper. "You ride?"

Cooper shrugged. "Some."

Emma glanced sideways as he walked with her toward the barn. He'd slung the saddlebag over his naked shoulder and he looked even more rugged and appealing than ever.

What was wrong with her? She didn't *want* to like him, and she certainly didn't like that her brothers had completely given over the task of testing him to her. So be it. Emma squared her shoulders and marched into the barn, selected the biggest, baddest, orneriest horse on the ranch for Cooper to ride. Her brothers would see him get thrown, lose all respect and mark Cooper off the list of marriageable men for Emma.

A stab of guilt struck Emma as she led Diablo, the black stallion, out of his stall. The horse snorted and tugged against the lead rope. She'd just about decided to put him back when somebody stepped into the doorway to the barn, blocking the sunlight. By the way he stood with the saddlebag looped over his shoulder, there was no mistaking the person. Cooper moved deeper into the barn.

"Mine or yours?" he asked.

Emma started to say hers, but then she'd have to ride Diablo and the last time she had, she'd ended up in the emergency room with a broken rib. Ace and Colton liked riding him because he was a challenge and gave them some much needed practice bronc riding for when they got a wild hair to do the rodeo circuit.

"I was just moving him to a different stall." She couldn't, with a clear conscience, let Cooper ride Diablo. What if he got seriously injured just mounting the high-spirited stallion? "I think you should ride Jack. He's calm and has a smooth gait."

"What's wrong with this one?" Cooper took the lead rope and ran his hand over the stallion's neck.

Diablo's nostrils flared and he pawed the dirt.

"He takes a bit more to manage than a pleasant ride. I don't recommend him."

Cooper smiled at Emma, one side of his mouth hitching higher. "Don't think I can handle him?"

Her knees turned to mush. "I didn't say that. I don't know you that well, and I don't know how good a rider you are."

"What's his name?"

"Diablo," she said, her voice flat.

Cooper led the horse to the side and tied his lead. "Saddle?"

"In the tack room." Emma stood back, chewing her bottom lip. He was going along with her original plan. So why was she so upset? She'd tried to talk him out of riding Diablo, if he chose to ignore her, so be it. Emma shrugged and led Daisy, her palomino mare, out of her stall and slipped a blanket and saddle over her back.

Cooper tossed a blanket and saddle over the stallion's back like he'd done it before and with an ease that could only be from years of experience.

Emma slipped the bridle over Daisy's head and looped the reins over her neck. "I thought you lived in Dallas?"

"Outside Dallas. Not too far from here." Cooper lengthened the stirrup on the saddle and checked the tightness of the girth. "And you train horses? Thoroughbred or Quarter horses?"

"Both." Emma led Daisy past the stranger. "And you make a living by trading stock?"

"As it says in my dossier." He gathered Diablo's

reins and followed her out of the barn. "And you like to ride, hunt and fish."

"How do you stay in such great shape if you work at a desk all day long?"

"I don't."

"I'd say you're in shape."

He laughed, the sound a deep rumble in his bare chest. "I stay in shape, I don't work at a desk all day long. There are such things as mobile applications. For the most part, I work from wherever I happen to be."

Emma frowned. She'd have to have a talk with Leslie. Cooper was not at all what she'd asked for. Where was the pasty accountant with the geek glasses and spare tire around his middle?

Instead, she'd gotten a tall, dark and incredibly attractive man with enough confidence to give Diablo a try.

Thank goodness for Diablo, he'd be the clincher. And she didn't feel a bit bad about it. Cooper had insisted after she'd warned the man.

Out in the barnyard, her brothers worked at unloading the bales of hay into a pole barn nearby.

When Emma and Cooper emerged, Colton stopped what he was doing, mouth agape. "You're not letting him ride Diablo, are you?"

Ace, Brand and Dillon all came to stand with Colton. "Emma, you know how that stallion is."

"He's a regular ball-buster. Let me get you a riding

horse." Dillon stepped toward the barn.

"No, it's okay. Emma warned me Diablo has some quirks."

Ace snorted. "Quirks? Is that what she told you?"

"Something like that." Cooper looped the reins over the horse's neck and grabbed the saddle horn, stuck his boot in the stirrup and swung up on Diablo.

No sooner had his full weight hit the saddle than the horse launched his offensive. Diablo arched his back and bounced like a pogo stick around the barnyard in bone-rattling jolts.

Emma's brothers hooted.

"Ride 'em, Cooper!" Brand shouted.

"Eight seconds, that's all you need." Ace grinned and waved his cowboy hat.

"Show him who's boss," Colton said.

As the horse spun and changed directions, Dillon grimaced. "Hang on, cowboy."

Emma cringed and waited. Invariably, Diablo tossed his rider within four seconds.

Cooper had already gone five and the guys were counting.

"Six seconds."

"Seven."

"Eight."

Then Cooper flew into the air over the horse's head, did a full somersault and rolled right back up on his feet.

The Jacob brothers applauded, while Dillon

snagged Diablo's reins as the horse bolted for the barn.

"Good job, Coop." Ace pounded him on the back.

"Got more balls than I do." Colton grinned and held out his hand to clasp Cooper's.

Shaking her head, Emma moaned, "This is not happening."

"He's good." Dillon hugged her, his grin grating on Emma's last nerve. "Eight seconds more than most guys who mount Diablo."

"We're not done yet." In case Emma thought things couldn't get worse, Cooper snatched Diablo's reins and walked him away from the crowd of Jacobs men, speaking quietly to the spooked horse.

As Diablo was led away, his eyes were wide, his nostrils flaring and he was breathing hard from having bucked off Cooper. He pranced sideways, tugging against the tight hold Cooper had on the reins.

"What's he doing?" Dillon asked Emma.

"Hell if I know." Emma frowned and waited, holding Daisy's reins.

"You done good, sis." Dillon nodded toward Cooper. "The man's strong, ain't afraid of hard work and likes a challenge."

"You could do a lot worse," Colton added.

"Really? The man's insane to even try riding Diablo once." As she said the words, Emma gasped. "Someone better call 9-1-1, he's up again."

"Holy hell, look at him," Ace whispered.

No hoots and hollers this time. All five Jacobs stood transfixed as Cooper leaned over Diablo's neck, talking quietly in his ear.

The horse whickered softly, but his ears remained perked, not pinned backward like they had been while bucking.

"I'd never believe it if I hadn't seen it with my own eyes," Brand said.

Emma gulped, her heart beating hard against her ribs as Cooper nudged Diablo, sending him trotting over to the gathered brothers.

"Are you leading the way?" Cooper smiled down at Emma.

Emma stared up into the clearest blue eyes she'd ever seen, the twinkle in them magnified by the bright shine of his white smile. Awareness tugged deep in her belly. Damn. She was in big trouble. "Y-yes. I'll lead the way." This "disaster date" wasn't turning out like she'd plan.

Colton leaned close and whispered in her ear, "Don't screw this one up, sis. We like him."

Emma mounted her horse and set off across the pasture at a gallop, without looking back. Maybe she'd get lucky and Diablo would regain his horrible reputation in time to salvage her attempt to sabotage her date. If not, she would have to follow through on her flippant suggestion of skinny-dipping in the creek.

CHAPTER 3

His SHOULDERS ACHED from the hours of hard work tossing up hay bales onto the trailer and his right knee hurt like the devil from being thrown by his mount, but Cooper couldn't hold back the grin spreading across his face. Hell, this was the most interesting, and perhaps best, first date he'd ever experienced.

He knew as soon as the Jacobs men stepped up to greet him that he was in for some kind of test to prove he was worthy of taking out their sister. He'd felt good he was up to the challenge and managed to gain the brothers' approval.

Since first seeing Emma walk down the steps from the house, he'd been more than taken by her fresh, sun-kissed appearance. He'd caught her staring at him more than once after he'd shed his shirt while hauling hay. Each time, her face had reddened and her pretty green eyes widened. She hadn't flirted and she'd been a bit standoffish. Rather than irritate, her odd behavior intrigued him.

Not only were her brothers challenging him, by her hot and cold signals, Emma had challenged him in a way he found exhilarating. Even her invitation to swim in the nude in the creek had been thrown down like a gauntlet, probably to get under her brothers' skin. By damn, Cooper was going to take her up on the dare.

If nothing else, he'd push her to the edge and see what Emma Jacobs was made of. She and her brothers had tested him—time to see if Emma Jacobs measured up. Was she truly his perfect match as Leslie and her confounded computerized match-maker claimed?

After Cooper had calmed Diablo and gotten him to behave, the ride to the creek passed in silence. Still sticky from sweating and covered in dirt and hay dust, Cooper couldn't wait to plunge into the pool. He followed behind Emma, admiring the way she held herself straight in the saddle and rode with fluid grace and dignity. Never once had she glanced back.

Something was bothering her and Cooper had a feeling he was the cause. A smile tugged at his lips. He hadn't felt this good in a long time and the sensation had to do with this woman and her well-meaning brothers. How nice to be a part of a family who cared enough about each other to take the time to check out a potential mate for one of their own.

Cooper had grown up an only child of elderly parents. When they'd died in a car wreck, he'd been shuttled from one foster home to another, never staying long enough to become a part of the family and always wishing he was. Emma was truly fortunate to have so many brothers to look out for her.

The woman led him over hills, through several ordinary farm gates, one marked *No Trespassing*, and down into a long, green valley. A stream burbled at the center of the valley, surrounded by tall willows and cypress trees. She passed through a stand of red oak trees and reined in at a point where the creek widened into a pool the size of a lunging corral. Big enough to get wet all over, yet small enough to be intimate and leave little to the imagination should they both get naked and swim together.

Not only was Cooper hot and sweaty, but now his jeans were too tight and chafing where he sat in the saddle. Even if Emma wasn't getting in, he sure as hell planned on taking advantage of the pool's soothing waters. Maybe swimming would tamp down his surging desire for the woman who refused to look him straight in the eye.

Emma slid from her mount, her gaze shooting back toward the trail she'd taken into the copse of trees.

"Expecting someone?" Cooper dropped to the

ground and tied his horse to a tree branch in the shade of a willow.

"I thought my brothers..." Her cheeks flamed. "That is...they usually..." Her brows furrowed and she walked a few steps back the way they'd come, peering through the tree branches. "Of all the times to actually grant me a little privacy, they had to choose this one."

"Excuse me?" Cooper tossed his shirt on a tree branch. "Were they going to join us?"

"They usually do." Emma's frown deepened. "But apparently not today."

"And that bothers you?" Cooper fought the grin threatening to break loose, schooling his face to seriousness. "I promise not to attack you, if that's what you're afraid of."

She cast him a brief glance, her lips twisting. "I can take care of myself." Emma returned to her horse and reached out, her fingers working at the ties on the saddlebag.

"I'd just as soon swim before I eat, if it's all right by you." Cooper toed off his boots, pulled off his socks and stood barefoot on the gravel. "Are you coming in?"

"Look, Mr. Johnson."

"Cooper. I thought we were past the formalities."

Emma planted her hands on her hips and finally faced him. "You should know, I only agreed to go out on this date to get my brothers to back off in their efforts to find me a husband."

Cooper nodded. So that was her game. Now her actions all made sense. "And how's that working for you?"

Her lips twisted into a frown. "Not so good. I thought you'd be a geek, a desk jockey with a pasty face and the soft hands of an accountant. My brothers would have run you off the ranch in the first five minutes."

"Your plan."

"Yes. Then they'd finally quit shoving men in my face. I'm happy the way I am. I don't need a man in my life, and I just wish they'd accept that and let me be."

"So, I was supposed to fail their man-tests and go home scared to ask you out on a second date?"

"Yes." She sighed and her shoulders slumped. "I'm sorry. I know Leslie's trying to get her business going and the fact her computer hooked me up with you should have been a good thing for you and her business. Frankly, my intentions were not to find my future mate."

"You only wanted a decoy to distract your brothers." Cooper crossed his arms over his chest then raised a hand to cup his chin. "Sorry to disappoint."

"No offense, but..." She reached out and touched his arm.

What could only be described as an electric

current shot through Cooper's arm, ripping through his body like a lightning bolt, then angling downward to make his dusty jeans even tighter.

Emma's eyes widened and she jerked back her hand.

Cooper cleared his throat and forced himself to ignore the current between them. "But what?"

She blinked and tipped her head upward to stare into his eyes. "But what?"

"You were saying no offense, but..." Cooper almost laughed at her obvious confusion.

Damn, she must have felt the connection too. So much so, that the sensation had thrown her off her original train of thought.

"Oh, yes, yes...No offense, but I've been in love, and I don't relish going there again."

"He dumped you, huh?"

Her back stiffened and she drew away, her eyes shooting sparks. "No, he died."

The words hit Cooper hard in the gut and he wished he could retract his hurtful remark. "I'm sorry. I didn't know."

She sighed, her green eyes darker, sadder. Emma turned away, wrapping her arms around her middle. "Two years ago, he was killed in Afghanistan. We were supposed to get married when he returned."

Cooper's chest tightened. Before he'd realized it, he'd closed the distance between them and wrapped his arms around her, drawing her back against his chest. "And your brothers think you should get over it and move on."

She laughed, the sound more of a sob, twisting a sharp-edged knife into Cooper's heart. But she didn't pull away from his touch this time. "Yeah. Only how do you get over losing the love of your life? It's not like you can replace him with someone else. My brothers mean well, they just don't get that."

"So, I'm supposed to throw them off." He turned her to face him, a plan forming. One he couldn't believe he was about to initiate. "How about this? We pretend to date a couple times to get your brothers on board, then I break it off with some lame excuse. You pretend to be hurt and your brothers leave you alone to get over the break up." As soon as he said the words, he knew without a doubt, he was making a mistake. A big one. But the way she looked upward with those soulful, sad, green eyes and her girl-next-door fresh-faced look, he couldn't just walk away and tell Leslie her program sucked. He'd see this through and hoped, in the meantime, he didn't make the bigger mistake of falling in love with a woman whose heart was taken by a dead man.

EMMA RESTED her hands on Cooper's bare chest, her momentary lapse into morose sorrow being quickly replaced by an awareness of the man holding her in his strong arms. "You'd do that for me?"

He nodded. "I wouldn't have offered, if I didn't mean it."

Her brows knotted. "What's in this deal for you?"

He shrugged. "Someone to go to dinner with a couple times. A picnic and a swim in what looks like a cool and inviting pool." He jerked his chin toward the water.

"Are you sure? Doesn't sound like a good deal to me." Her gaze roved over his face and broad shoulders, her heart rate kicking up a notch. "Who are you trying to kid? Any woman would give their best stilettos to go out with a guy like you."

"Yeah, but I don't like leaving dates up to chance. I'd rather go out with someone I know."

"But you don't know me."

"You like horses, hunting and fishing. I don't know many girls who like to do half of that."

"And that makes me okay in your book?" Emma laughed.

"Well, you're easy on the eye. Tall, slender, nice hair." He lifted her braid and let it slip through his fingers.

His intense gaze made Emma hot all over, something she couldn't get used to. Still, his offer held merit. "I guess it'll work. But I don't want to take advantage of you."

"Like you weren't already?" He clucked his tongue. "Seriously, Emma."

She liked the way her name rolled off his tongue,

raising gooseflesh across her skin. To dispel the feeling, she rubbed her arms. "Yeah, but you didn't know I was using you."

"So, it's okay to take advantage when I'm clueless, but not when I'm fully aware?"

She smiled, her first real smile since Cooper showed up.

"You know, you're not half bad to look at, when you smile." He chucked her beneath the chin.

"Thanks." Her lips quirked. "I think."

"So, is it a deal?" He held out his hand.

"We'll pretend to date?"

"Right."

Her eyes narrowed again. "No...physical expectations?"

"Not unless you want to."

"I don't," she blurted. Her cheeks heated and her heart skipped several beats then raced on at the thought of making love with this man. Not that she'd act on that thought. That was the whole point to this charade. She stuck out her hand. "Then I guess we have a deal."

Cooper took it. "Deal." Instead of shaking it, he tugged hard enough to pull her against his chest.

"What are you doing?" Emma whispered, her body pressed into his, fire burning through her veins.

"This deal should be sealed with a kiss."

Before she could protest, he bent and claimed her lips, in a brief, but no less earth-moving, kiss.

When he lifted his head, he smiled down at her. "That's better."

"I thought we agreed, no physical expectations." She pushed against his chest.

"Oh, well, it's a done deal and I can't take it back." He shrugged and loosened his hold. "Now, can I get in the pool and rinse off the dust?"

Her lips still tingling and heat suffusing parts of her body she'd thought long cooled, Emma nodded. "You didn't need my permission."

"Good, because I'm all in." He reached for the rivet on his jeans.

Emma's eyes widened, her gaze fixed on Cooper's hand. "What are you doing?"

"You said a swimsuit wasn't required, and I don't relish swimming in my jeans. I tend to sink like a rock in denim." He whipped down the zipper, and stepped free.

Holy hell, the man went commando beneath his jeans. Emma's cheeks heated and she turned her back, but not before she caught a glimpse of a dark thatch of hair and a rock-hard... "Geez, at least give me a little warning," she gasped.

His jeans flew past her to land on a tree branch.

Out of the corner of her eye, Emma watched him enter the water, his narrow hips and tight buttocks absolute male perfection.

Her heart thumped hard, reminding her that despite having lost the love of her life, she was still very much alive and appreciative of a fine male form.

A niggle of guilt tamped down the rush of lust threatening to overwhelm her senses. She'd loved her fiancé, more than life itself. Then why was she attracted to this man?

Her inner devil answered. What wasn't to admire about a man whose body was comprised of long fluid lines and taut muscles?

A splash behind her made her turn.

Cooper surfaced and stood waist-deep in the water, covering all the important parts. He grinned and waved a beckoning hand. "Feels great. Aren't you coming in?"

"Y-yes. In a moment." She faced him, giving him a stern glare. "And only if you don't watch."

"I'll even turn around if it makes you more comfortable."

"Yes. Do."

He turned his back to her.

She reached for the hem of her shirt and pulled it over her torso, pausing halfway up. What was she thinking? Getting naked and swimming in a pool with Cooper could lead to only one thing.

If she let it.

"How do I know you won't take advantage of me?" she called out.

"I don't make it a habit of raping my dates. I only make love to *willing* women." His tone was flat.

What did she have to lose? She was hot, sweaty and the pool did look inviting. She whipped the T-shirt over her head and tossed it over a tree branch. Her hand paused on the catches of her bra. She could leave on her underwear. What was a swimsuit anyway but colorful underwear? Unfortunately, she'd chosen white lace for her bra and panties, they would have to do.

Emma shimmied out of her jeans and stood in the thin panties and bra, the warm air caressing her skin. "No peeking."

Cooper chuckled. "No promises."

She hurried toward the water, splashing in as Cooper turned to face her.

"Feels good, doesn't it?" he said.

"Always." Emma kept her distance, grateful the shadows cast by the trees hid everything beneath the water. She swam past him and turned onto her back to float, closing her eyes to the bright sun shining through the gaps in the branches.

Movement beside her made her open her eyes.

Cooper floated on his back alongside her, his chest rising out of the water, droplets gleaming against his tanned skin.

Emma's gaze skimmed over his chest and down to his taut abs and lower where a dark line of hair arrowed toward... She gasped, her mouth filling with water, and her body sank. She came up sputtering, and flailing, the water too deep for her to stand.

Strong, calloused hands gripped around her waist and held her above the water until she coughed the liquid from her lungs and she could breathe.

"You all right?"

"Yes," she said, and coughed. He stood so close, her thighs touched his and his member bumped against her belly. Fire ignited low in her belly, spreading even lower. "I'm okay now, you can let go."

For a long moment, he held her, his fingers tightening on her arms, his blue-eyed gaze burning into hers.

Her breath caught and held. Cooper was going to kiss her. Her lips tingled in anticipation of tasting his again. Without thinking, she leaned toward him, her eyelids lowering, her gaze fixed on those incredibly sexy lips.

Then he let go and stepped away.

Down she went again, her head dipping beneath the surface. At least this time, her mouth was closed. The shock of a near miss on a kiss made her want to stay below the surface until the water cooled her cheeks and lowered the temperature of her entire body. By the time she came up, her lungs were starving for air and she was still hot and bothered.

Yup, being in a pool with a naked Cooper Johnson wasn't helping her keep a cool head.

But apparently, he had no problem keeping away. He swam to the far side of the pool, ducked beneath the water and disappeared.

Emma glanced around, searching for tell-tell ripples or bubbles. None appeared.

When she thought he'd been down long enough, she moved toward the position where he'd disappeared. Had he gotten stuck in the mud?

She'd only moved two feet when something snagged her ankle and yanked her down.

Emma jerked and kicked free, surfacing to suck in air.

Cooper came up beside her.

"No fair. I wasn't expecting that."

Cooper shook his head. "And you have brothers? Come on, Emma, you're not as tough as you put on."

Challenge made and accepted. Emma launched herself at his head, and pushed him under.

His arms circled her waist and he threw her into the air.

Emma came down with a huge splash, laughing and sputtering. She pushed him under and he tossed her several more times before she climbed up on a large boulder and stretched out, tired but smiling. She hadn't laughed or played with such abandon for a long time.

She gasped and her smile slipped from her face. She hadn't been that happy since Marcus left for the war. Not a day or hour had gone by since he left that Emma hadn't thought about Marcus.

Until today. She'd gone for hours, thinking about

Cooper instead of Marcus. Her chest tightened. That couldn't be.

Water splashed on her face, bringing her back to the present.

"Thinking of him?" Cooper's warm, husky tones rumbled beside her.

Emma opened one eye. "Yeah."

Cooper lay beside her on his belly, propped on his elbows. At least, one part of him wasn't dangling in the wind. Unfortunately, his glorious buttocks drew Emma's gaze like a magnet.

To keep from staring, she closed her eyes and pretended to relax. "You know my sob story now. What about you? Why aren't you married and herding a half-dozen children?"

For a long time, Cooper didn't respond.

Emma opened her eyes, wondering if he'd fallen asleep.

No. He stared into the shadows, his blue eyes glazed as if he looked into the past. "I grew up in foster homes. Some of them good, some not so good. I guess I didn't want to end up in a relationship that wasn't going to last. Plus, I've been too busy with my career to give time to making a relationship work."

"Sounds like you haven't met the right woman." Emma closed her eyes again, wondering who the right woman would be for Cooper. A little jab of envy twisted her gut. Whoever he chose to marry would be a lucky woman. As far as Emma had seen, the man was a gem. Hard-working, sensitive, smart and damned fine looking.

"Maybe," Cooper said.

"You don't strike me as a man who'd let a computerized matchmaker find your mate."

Cooper snorted. "I'm doing a friend a favor."

Emma turned on her side, fighting not to let her gaze travel below Cooper's waist. "I don't get it."

"Leslie is a friend of a friend. I volunteered for the program to help Leslie test her software and get her business off the ground." He shrugged. "I have to admit to being skeptical."

"And look what you got…" Emma sighed. "A woman who only wanted a date to get her brothers off her back." She pressed her lips together. "Look, don't let me deter you from trying again. Your girl is out there. And you'll know it when you find her."

"How do you know?"

"I knew when I met Marcus that he was the one for me."

"And you don't think you could fall in love again?"

"No." Her throat tightened. "We were like two halves to a whole. That perfection will never happen again."

"You're lucky."

"Lucky?" Emma choked on a sob. "Marcus is dead."

"Better to have loved and lost…" Cooper shrugged. "You know."

Emma smiled through a shimmer of tears and studied his profile. "You know, you really aren't half bad."

"Thanks." He tipped his head. "I think."

"No really. If I was open to loving again, I might be attracted to you." Man, was that a big fib. Emma lay back, and closed her eyes out of self defense, unable to keep her gaze from straying over Cooper's magnificent body. "You have a nice ass."

Cooper laughed out loud, the sound warming the air around Emma. She liked the sound of Cooper's laugh. It was completely different than Marcus's. Emma thought back, but at that moment, she couldn't quite remember how Marcus laughed. All she knew was that Cooper's laughter made her want to laugh with him.

"I guess I should feed you." She rolled away, disturbed by the idea that she couldn't remember Marcus's laughter. "If you're anything like my brothers, you could eat a side of beef in a sitting."

"Not quite that bad." His stomach gave a hollow growl. "Guess the hay hauling burned a few calories."

"Then come on." She stood. "On second thought, you can get dressed while I lay out our picnic. The least you should get out of our day together is a meal." And she'd be a lot better off once Cooper had his clothes on.

Once again, Emma turned her back to the man to allow him the privacy to dress. Ignoring him wasn't an option as Cooper passed Emma, walking tall and proud and completely naked, to fetch his jeans from the branch beside her.

And based on how straight and stiff his member was, he wasn't immune to her wearing just her bra and panties.

Holy hell, she'd stirred up a hornet's nest of desire in him. And if she was honest with herself, she was just as turned on.

She forced herself to think of Marcus and how he looked in his uniform as he'd kissed her goodbye at the airport.

Emma refused to acknowledge one glaring truth: memories of Marcus seemed much more faded than they had before the day began—before she'd met Cooper.

CHAPTER 4

TIRED AND STRANGELY CONTENT, Cooper rode into the barnyard beside Emma. He couldn't remember the last time he'd been on a picnic or swam nude in a creek, but the activities seemed so natural, giving him a feeling of home. Not a good thing, considering he'd agreed to date and then dump her. No use getting attached to Emma or her family if he wasn't to be a part of it.

Having grown up in the foster care system, he'd been careful not to let his heart get involved with his host family. If he hadn't been forced into a group project with a team of guys during his second year on campus at Texas A&M, he might still be scratching out a living. As part of their class assignment, they'd researched the stock market, pooled their pathetic financial resources and invested. By the end of the semester, they'd doubled their money and pulled an A in the class. Most importantly, they'd bonded and formed a club of four guys with the optimistic name of Billionaires Anonymous. Now these guys were the family he never had, the brothers he could count on if he was in a bind or just needed someone to talk to.

Until he'd passed through the gates of the Rockin' J Ranch, Cooper hadn't thought to expand his circle of friends. Now, he found himself wishing things had been different. He liked Emma's brothers. He liked Emma even more.

He tied Diablo to his stall door, removed the saddle and blanket and set them on a saddletree. "When did you want to go on our next date?"

Emma tugged the leather strap through the girth. "I don't know. In a couple days, maybe?"

Cooper reached over her and slid the saddle off the mare's back.

Emma frowned. "I can do that."

"I know." With a smile, Cooper settled the saddle on the rack next to his. He handed her a brush and touched the side of her cheek with his finger. "It's one of the things I like best about you."

"That I can lift a saddle?"

"That and your independent spirit."

"I thought most men liked women who needed to be protected."

"I'm not most men."

"You can say that again," she muttered, sliding the brush over the palomino's coat.

"What was that?" Cooper asked.

"Nothing," she replied as she stroked harder.

Cooper smiled. He'd heard her comment and his ego swelled just a little. The woman may not want a relationship, but she was aware of him. A step in the right direction, if he hoped to change her mind about giving him a chance.

His hand stopped in mid-stroke.

Did he want a chance with Emma?

She'd been up front about not wanting a relationship. He glanced over the stallion's back. Her long thick braid was still damp from their swim in the creek and her face was pink from the sun. Her hands moved over the horse with strong, sure strokes. She wasn't a girly girl and she wasn't afraid to break a nail or get dirty. An image of her in her white, lacy panties and bra had his groin tightening all over again. Beneath her tough exterior was a soft, warm and beautiful woman.

She straightened and leaned over the top of her horse. "Thanks for playing along with the boys today."

"Sorry the date didn't quite work out the way you wanted."

"That's okay. You didn't know. And we'll make the plan work."

Cooper finished off the stallion and led him to his stall.

Emma held out her hand for his brush.

Their fingers collided. Cooper felt that spark again and forced himself to drop his hands at his sides. He wanted to pull her into his arms and kiss her.

She stepped away and practically ran to the tack room to deposit the brushes. "I suppose you'd better say your goodbyes to my brothers." Emma led the way out of the barn and up to the house.

All four brothers sat on the back porch, feet up on the railing, sipping longneck bottles of beer.

Brand grinned. "How was the swim?"

"Great. Nice place y'all have here." Cooper pressed a hand to the small of Emma's back as they walked up the steps.

Once on the deck, she turned. "Thanks for the help hauling hay and for a nice picnic, Cooper." She leaned up on her toes and pressed a kiss to his cheek. "See ya in a few days?"

He bent his head and smiled, caught her around the waist and pulled her against him. "You can count on it." Then he lowered his lips to claim hers in a deep, soul-satisfying kiss.

Beside them, her brothers whooped.

At first stiff beneath his hands, Emma's muscles eventually slackened and she melted against him, her mouth opening to let his tongue slide in.

A rush of warmth filled Cooper's body and he forgot for a moment where he was.

"Eh-hem. Still here," Colton said.

"Yeah, could you keep it G-rated?" Ace chuckled. "You might offend Dillon."

"Seein' as he's still a virgin," Brand added.

Cooper broke off the kiss, heat rushing into his cheeks and places farther south.

"I'm headed in for a shower." Emma spun and ducked into the house. "Thanks again." The screen door slammed behind her.

Her boot heels clicked across the wooden floor, fading as she turned a corner.

"Well, Coop." Ace pushed to his feet. "Let me get you a beer." He ducked into the house.

"I really shouldn't," Cooper called out after him, thinking he needed to leave before the brothers noticed the bulge in his jeans.

Ace didn't respond, disappearing into the shadows of the interior.

"I probably should be headed back." Cooper glanced at his watch. "Takes a good thirty minutes to get home."

"What's your hurry?" Brand stood and draped an arm over Cooper's shoulder. "The Aggies game is on in ten minutes. You watch much football?"

"On occasion." His football scholarship with Texas A&M had been his ticket to a higher education and Cooper had made it count. He'd planned on watching the game after his date. If he left now, he'd only miss the first quarter.

"Then it's settled, you're staying for the game." Ace reappeared and shoved an ice-cold bottle into his hand.

Brand held open the door. "Come on. We can catch the tail-end of the commentaries."

Cooper stepped into the Jacobs' home, glancing at the hallway he was sure Emma had disappeared down, wondering what she'd say when she found him watching the game with her brothers. He shrugged. Since the guys had invited him, he guessed her opinion wouldn't matter. Not as if they were broken up or anything. Hell, they weren't officially together.

"I'll get the nachos." Colton turned toward what looked like the kitchen.

Cooper settled onto one end of a bomber-jacket brown leather couch.

The Jacobs brothers spread out around the room, all drinking bear, eating peanuts and nachos and commenting on the commentators until kickoff. Then the shouting began.

Before long, Cooper was shouting right along with them.

EMMA STOOD under the shower spray for longer than normal, letting the cool water chill the heat simmering low in her belly since Cooper had first taken off his shirt hauling hay and later, when he strode past her naked, flaunting his stiff...

She turned the handle to a cooler setting, trying to wash away the memory of Cooper's...tight abs and even tighter butt.

No matter how cold the water, she couldn't shake the burning in her belly. Thank goodness, she wouldn't have to see him for a few days. Maybe she'd tell him she couldn't see him at all. So what if her brothers kept setting her up with prospective husbands? At least, none of their attempts had made her feel as uncomfortable and sexually aware as Cooper Johnson had.

By the time her skin had pruned, Emma felt in reasonable control of her libido and she stepped from the shower, towel-dried her hair then wrapped it turban style.

Shouts from the living room made her smile. The Aggies must be playing. She hoped she hadn't missed anything. While most women she knew would rather spend a football afternoon out shopping, Emma enjoyed watching the game with her brothers. Marcus used to watch with them, although he preferred University of Texas over the Aggies. Emma hadn't held that against him.

She tossed her towel into the hamper, slipped into a baggy Aggies T-shirt that hung halfway down her thighs, grabbed a brush and padded barefoot into the living room. "Who's winning?" The words had barely left her lips when she spotted Cooper, and the heat she'd fought to cool flamed all over again.

The Aggies defense snagged an interception and ran for a goal.

All five men shouted at once, pumping fists in the air and high-fiving each other.

Cooper glanced over his shoulder. "Aggies are up fourteen to ten."

Ace patted the seat beside him. "Sit. You're missing a great game." No sooner had he said the words, his attention returned to the game.

The seat Ace patted happened to be on the couch, between Ace and Cooper. Emma glanced down at her shirt and remembered her hair was still in wet tangles. "I should go put on some more clothes, since we have company."

"Just Cooper. You two went skinny-dipping. You're wearing more now than you were then." Brand snorted. "Girls."

"Since you're up, could you make some popcorn?" Colton asked.

"And bring us a fresh round of beer," Dillon added.

"What am I, your maid?" She fisted her hand around her brush and propped it on her hip, glaring at her brothers.

"Well, now that you mention it..." Brand grinned

and ducked as her brush sailed through the air, aimed at his head. "Hey! Watch it."

"Right, next time I won't miss." She shook her head, a smile replacing her glare. "Men." She spun on her bare heel and headed for the kitchen, glad for the respite from sitting on the sofa with Cooper. She could deliver the requested popcorn and beer and make some excuse to return to her room for the rest of the evening.

She really thought her plan would work. Until...

"Where do I put the empties?" Cooper's deep voice said behind her.

Emma had been in the process of opening the box with the popcorn when Cooper walked in. Her hand jerked and the individually wrapped popcorn bags flew across the room. "Holy hell."

Cooper set the empty beer bottles on the counter and dropped to his haunches, his hand closing around the same bag Emma grabbed.

She jerked back her hand, her eyes wide as a shot of electricity bolted up her arm and that crazy heat singed her insides.

Cooper chuckled. "I didn't mean to startle you."

"It's okay. The bottles go in the corner trash can." She hoped he'd take the hint and leave her to pick up her mess. Alone.

Instead, he gathered two other packages and the box and handed them to her.

Their fingers brushed together and Emma almost

threw the box again. She jerked upward at the same time as Cooper, crashing foreheads. Pain arrowed through Emma's skull, making her stagger backward.

"Here." Cooper slipped an arm around her waist. "Lean on me. That had to hurt. I've been known to have a hard head."

Forced to accept his offer or fall on her ass, Emma leaned into his muscled chest and blinked her eyes until the gray fog around the edges cleared.

Cooper's fresh, outdoorsy scent overwhelmed her senses, and the warmth of his hand on the small of her back sent shivers of awareness across her skin. All that stood between his hand and her skin was a T-Shirt.

As soon as the thought registered, Emma pushed away. "Why are you still here?" she demanded, relying on anger to hide the confusing signals her body was sending to her brain.

He grinned. "Your brothers invited me to watch the game."

Emma shoved a bag in the microwave and jammed her finger on the correct button then faced him, her hands fisted on her hips. "So?"

He shrugged. "I'd planned on watching it at my house, but our date ran a little longer than expected." Cooper held up his hands. "Not that I was disappointed. I have to say skinny-dipping in the creek was the highlight of the day. I wouldn't have missed it for a game."

Her cheeks heated and she snorted. "Well, don't get too cozy. Our arrangement is only temporary."

"Do you want me to leave?" His brows rose up his forehead.

Hell yes, she wanted him to leave. His very presence made her twitchy, confused and...damn it...horny! "No. That would be too obvious. You might as well stay for the rest of the game."

He tipped his head, his lips twisting. "Thanks...I think."

"If you'll grab the beer, I'll bring the popcorn."

"Yes, ma'am." He gave her a mocking salute, dumped the empty bottles in the trash and pulled five bottles from the fridge. "You sure I can't help you here?"

"No," she said, the word a little harsher than she'd intended. What was wrong with her? She was never this rude to guests. She added in a softer tone. "I can handle this."

His lips tipped upward. "You sure?"

Emma's gaze captured Cooper's. "Positive."

As soon as he left the kitchen, Emma sagged against the counter. Who was she kidding? She could handle the popcorn. It was the man who had her belly turning cartwheels. The sooner their deal was over, the sooner she could get back to normal.

COOPER HANDED out the round of beer and settled on

the couch, sure to leave room for Emma between him and Ace. With all the other chairs taken by her hulking brothers, she'd have only one choice. Based on her reaction in the kitchen, his presence was causing her some discomfort. Hopefully, in a good way and in his favor.

The scent of seasoned popcorn filled the air.

Cooper settled back on the sofa in an attempt to appear casual and focused on the game when all he could think about was Emma and the sexy curve of her thighs as her T-shirt brushed across them with every step she took.

Then she was there, carrying a bowl full of fluffy hot popcorn, her hair still tangled and damp.

She handed the popcorn to Colton, snatched up her brush and turned to leave.

Ace patted the seat beside him. "Sit. I'll brush while we watch the game."

Her gaze went from the space on the couch next to Cooper and then the game.

At that moment, the A&M quarterback spun a thirty-yard pass.

Emma's eyes widened and her face grew intense.

When the receiver caught the ball, he ran for another twenty yards before being tackled on the twenty-yard line.

"Come on, you can't leave now." Ace held out his hand.

Emma slapped the brush into her brother's palm,

dropped to the floor in front of him and lifted her long hair off her neck.

Cooper missed the touchdown for watching Ace as he brushed his sister's hair.

After only six strokes, Ace handed Cooper the brush. "Gotta make a pit stop. Wanna take over?" He leaped from his seat and made a beeline for the center hallway.

Emma glared at her retreating brother, then faced Cooper with her hand extended. "I can do it myself."

He held the brush out of her reach and slid down to the end of the sofa, positioning his knees on either side of her shoulders. "I don't mind."

"But I might," she whispered.

Cooper leaned close and spoke into her ear. "Consider it part of your plan." Then he lifted a strand of already drying hair and worked the brush through the tangles, easing out the snarls without tugging on the roots

"Ummm." The starch washed out of Emma's shoulders the more Cooper brushed.

Ace dropped onto the couch a few moments later. "I can take over again."

"Uh uh," Emma said. "Cooper's much better at it. At least, he isn't yanking all the hair out of my head."

Ace patted Cooper's back. "A man of many talents. I take it you have sisters?"

Cooper's chest tightened as he lifted another strand of hair and worked the brush through it.

"Nope. But I've brushed enough horse's tails to know how to work out a knot."

Dillon guffawed. "Hear that, Em? He's comparing you to a horse."

Emma glared back at Cooper.

Colton laughed out loud. "Not making points, are ya, buddy?"

"A bit rusty at romance, cowboy?" Emma queried.

"Just the facts, ma'am." Cooper planted his hand on her head and turned it back to the game. "The Aggies just scored."

"Something you won't do at this rate, huh, Coop?" Brand winked at Emma.

Emma tossed a pillow at her brother, her face bright pink. "Shut up, all of you. I'm trying to watch the game."

Even after he'd worked out all the tangles, Cooper couldn't bring himself to stop brushing Emma's hair. The game went on and Emma shouted a couple times when the quarterback threw an interception or the kicker missed a field goal. On those occasions, she leaned right or left, her shoulders bumping against the insides of Cooper thighs.

The contact made his body react in ways it shouldn't in the same room as Emma's four strapping hulks of brothers.

At one point, Emma handed Cooper his beer and he downed the last half in one gulp, hoping to take the edge off his growing lust. Nothing seemed to help. Emma was not only beautiful, but she liked sports and rode horses like a natural. The perfect woman as far as Cooper was concerned.

Her only drawback was that she was still in love. With a dead man. A war hero, at that. How could Cooper compete with a memory?

CHAPTER 5

BY THE TIME COOPER LEFT, they'd all had supper together, feasting on the steaks her brothers grilled and baked potatoes Emma shoved into the microwave. If anyone else had viewed the scene, they looked like one big happy family.

Emma knew different. That night, she crawled into bed and lay on her side, staring at the picture on her nightstand.

"Marcus, why did you have to die? If you were still here, this whole date thing wouldn't be an issue. By now, we'd be married and have a baby or two on the way." At the thought of her belly growing with child, her chest ached with a hollowness she couldn't fill. She and Marcus had wanted four children. Two boys and two girls. Heck, they'd have taken anything God had seen fit to give them. But that hadn't been in His plan.

Emma sighed and closed her dry eyes. After the initial shock of Marcus's death, she'd refused to shed another tear. Tears were for weak women, not Emma. A soft breeze lifted the filmy curtains around the open window. At times like this, she could almost feel Marcus touch her shoulder and reassure her everything would be all right. He'd had a way of gentling horses and people that Emma had never mastered and always appreciated.

Her last thought as she drifted off to sleep was not of Marcus, but of the dark-haired, blue-eyed blind-date she'd spent the day with. An image of him rising out of the water, completely naked, filled her last waking thought and sent her into dreams so erotic she tossed and turned throughout the night.

By five o'clock in the morning, she'd given up on sleep, slipped into her jeans and boots and headed to the barn. After a long ride across the pasture, greeting the morning sun, she found herself pulling to a halt at Willow Creek where she and Cooper had been skinny dipping the day before. Heat rose in her body before the sun's rays could warm the ground.

"Damn." She reined her horse around and rode hard all the way back to the barn, brushed and settled her horse in a stall and headed for the house, entering through the kitchen.

"Up kinda early, aren't you?" Ace stood at the stove, frying bacon. "Want a couple of eggs?"

"I'm not hungry." She grabbed a glass, poured it half full of orange juice and downed it in one gulp.

Ace flipped the bacon, his back to her. "Love has a way of ruining your appetite."

Anger surged and Emma slammed the glass on the counter. "I'm not in love. I only just met Cooper."

Ace shot a glance over his shoulder, a grin spreading across his face. "But he got under your skin, didn't he?"

"Why can't you guys get it through your thick skulls?" She tossed back her wind-tangled hair and braced her hands on her hips. "I loved Marcus and I'll never forget him. No other banker, insurance salesman or cowboy will ever take his place. Got that?"

Ace moved the pan off the burner and turned off the stove before gripping Emma's arms. "I know." He smoothed a hair out of her face. "You miss him. We get that. We're not asking you to stop loving him or forget him. We just want you to get on with your life and be happy."

"I'm as happy as I can be without Marcus." Emma stared up into Ace's eyes, her own so dry, she blinked. "Why can't you leave me alone?"

Ace smiled. "Because you're *not* happy. You're still hurting and living an empty life. It breaks our hearts that you're not willing to think there might be someone else out there for you."

She sniffed. "Marcus was the only man for me."

"Emma, you're young, and you have a big heart with a lot of room to love. I mean look at this family." He waved his hand over his head. "It's big. Four brothers is a lot for a girl to handle, but you love us all."

"That's different." She shoved a hand through her tangled hair. "You're family."

"How does a mother love more than one child?"

"Again, you're talking family."

"And you didn't consider Marcus family?"

Emma frowned. "Yes. Again, it's different. I wanted to marry him and have his children. I don't want to marry *you* or have *your* children." She shrugged.

"A comforting thought. But that's the beauty of the heart—it knows no limits. You have to give your-self a chance."

"You mean give *Cooper* a chance." She snorted and shook her head. "He's just another cowboy." Who'd set her blood burning through her veins when it had no business doing that.

"If not Cooper, someone else." Ace tipped her chin and stared into her eyes. "You can't make a future for yourself until you loosen your hold on the past. Marcus is dead. He'd have wanted you to move on. To find love again and have a family."

"I have all the family I need." She wrapped her arms around Ace's waist and buried her face in his shirt. "Why do I need more?" she muttered against his shirt.

"Because you deserve to love again." Ace patted her hair and held her close.

"Hey, what's all this hugging? Can a brother get in on some of that?" Brand entered the room, carrying his boots, his hair standing on end. He dropped the boots and opened his arms, wrapping them around Emma's back, sandwiching her between himself and Ace. "Never too early for a group hug, in my book."

"Can you lighten up?" Emma laughed. "I can't breathe."

Colton entered, fully dressed, clean-shaven and headed straight for the stove, bypassing Ace, Emma and Brand. "Watcha burnin'?"

"My bacon." Ace broke the hold and lunged for the pan. "If you want some, cook it yourself."

"Why, when you made enough for me?" Colton snitched a piece from the pan and popped it into his mouth, staring at Emma as he chewed. "Are we talking about Cooper?"

"No." Emma pulled the bacon package out of the fridge and slapped it on the counter. "We're low on sweet feed for the horses. Colton, why don't you head to the feed store after breakfast?"

"I'll go." Dillon entered the room, buttoning his chambray shirt.

"No, I'll do it." Colton pulled the carton of eggs

out of the refrigerator. "You'd get too busy flirting with Bekka and forget to bring home the feed."

Dillon's face reddened. "Would not."

"Would not what?" Colton grinned. "Forget or flirt?"

Dillon glared. "Either."

Emma shook her head. Dillon had it bad for Bekka Jones, the daughter of the feed store owner. "Why don't you ask her out?"

"She's got a boyfriend."

"Since when has that ever stopped you?" Brand shoved the loaf of bread into Dillon's hands. "Here, make yourself useful while I set the table."

Dillon grabbed a handful of bread from the bag and popped it into the toaster. "Emma's stalling. From what I could tell, you were talking about Cooper, not Bekka. Stick to the topic."

"We're not talking about Cooper," Emma insisted, her cheeks warming. "Do you want breakfast, or not?"

"Has he called yet?" Dillon asked.

Emma flipped her hair over her shoulder, her hand trembling just a bit. "Who?"

"You know who." Brand shook his head. "Cooper."

"No." With her back to the room, Emma refused to face the brother inquisition. "Why should he?"

"He said he was gonna ask our baby sister out on a proper date." Brand grinned. "Guess hauling hay, skinny dippin' and a football game isn't proper in his books."

Emma's fingers slipped on the greasy bacon and she dropped a piece on the counter. She had to remind herself, Cooper asking her on a date was all part of the plan. Stretching the bacon across the bottom of the pan, she sucked in a calming breath and let it out.

"Sounds like a good date to me." Colton cracked eggs into a second skillet. "Especially the skinny dippin' part."

"It would." Dillon punched his brother's shoulder. "Might explain why you don't have a girlfriend."

"I could have a girlfriend, if I wanted," Colton grumbled. "Just haven't met the right one."

"You know, instead of trying to marry me off to any ol' Tom, Dick or Harry, why aren't you boys settling down?" Emma plunked the pan of bacon on the burner and turned up the fire beneath it. She faced her brothers. "Why aren't you all married and making babies?"

Brand's brows rose. "Now, now. Don't change the subject. We were talking about you."

"Yeah, and I'm tired of that subject." She poked a finger into Brand's chest. "Why aren't you dating?"

"Yeah." Ace crossed his arms. "Why aren't you dating?"

Brand's brows drew together. "You're the oldest. Seems you should be the first to marry."

Dillon and Colton joined Brand in a line, arms crossed and all staring at Ace.

Emma hid her smile and turned back to the pan of sizzling bacon. Nothing like a little bait and switch to get her brothers off her back.

Breakfast continued with good-natured ribbing, the heat off Emma for the moment.

Though knowing Cooper would be calling her some time that day didn't help her nerves. Thank goodness, she had a job that would keep her away from the phone for most of the day. At the T-Bar M Ranch, she went through the day on autopilot, putting the horses through their paces, mucking stalls and grooming. By the time she got home, she was hungry and ready for a shower and a cool drink.

As she stepped into the house, the phone rang, sending her nerves skittering across her senses. Dillon had gone with Colton to town late in the afternoon. Emma had left Ace and Brand outside, adjusting the hinges on the gate to the corral, which left her alone in the house.

She let the phone ring once, twice...fully intending to let the answering machine pick up. But on the third ring, Ace entered the house.

"I'll get it." He picked up on the fourth ring before the answering machine.

Emma groaned and headed for the bathroom.

"Hey, Emma, it's for you," Ace called out.

Brand entered the door at that time. "Must be Coop. Say hello for me."

Emma trudged toward the hall phone where Ace held the receiver, a grin spreading across his face. "He wants to go out tonight. I told him you didn't have plans."

With a glare, Emma yanked the phone from Ace's hand. "Thanks."

"Be nice, Emma, or you'll scare him off."

She covered the mouthpiece and whispered, "That's the idea."

Ace snorted. "Even if you don't want to give him a chance, give yourself a chance. Go out for a change. You've been glued to the house since—" Her brother stopped before saying it. His eyes widened. "Sorry."

Emma's hand shook. She hadn't gone out at night since Marcus left for Afghanistan over two year ago, preferring the company of her brothers than running into well-wishers in town.

Ace grinned. "Oh, by the way, I was just kidding. It's not Cooper." He slipped away, leaving Emma to answer the phone.

She had words prepared to tell Cooper she didn't want to see him again. She didn't realize until Ace mentioned it that the caller would be anyone else. "This is Emma."

"Emma! Leslie here." The woman didn't wait to breathe before jumping in. "How was your date with Mr. Johnson?"

Great, sexy, everything most girls could want. "Not what I asked for," Emma replied in a flat tone.

"Oh." Leslie paused. "You didn't like him?"

Before responding, Emma glanced around to make sure her brothers were out of earshot. "I didn't want the date to work. I wanted it to be a complete failure to throw my brothers off my back."

"I knew it." A chuckle erupted into the phone. "You liked Cooper, didn't you?"

Emma leaned against the wall and closed her eyes. "That's beside the point."

"No, it's exactly the right point. My software worked and paired you with a perfect match."

Emma opened her eyes and stared out the front door to the Texas landscape. "My perfect match died."

"Honey, you have to let Marcus go," Leslie said softly. "He wouldn't have wanted you to mourn him for the rest of your life."

"You aren't listening, Leslie." Emma pushed a hand through her hair and lowered her voice. "I don't want another man in my life."

"You have to move on."

"Like you have?" Emma said, her voice a little harsher than necessary. Immediately she felt awful. "I'm sorry. That wasn't called for."

"You're right, Emma. I plan on moving on. I've entered my data into the program and I'm waiting for a match. I don't have all that many men entered into the system yet. But when the match comes along, I'll be...open-minded."

Emma sighed. "Maybe I'm just not ready."

"When are we ever? Getting back out in the dating market is scary. I get that." Leslie paused again. "Give Cooper a chance."

Boy, if that wasn't an echo, Emma didn't know what was. "You sound like my brothers."

"They liked him, too?" Leslie squealed. "I knew it!"

"Don't get all excited. I've already told Cooper I plan to ditch him. He's on board."

"Oh." Leslie's voice dropped an octave. "I'm sorry to hear that."

"I know you wanted to prove out your program, but I warned you, I'm not the right person."

"Cooper seemed like such a nice guy. I just knew you two would hit it off."

Oh, they had. But Emma wasn't telling Leslie that. With her brothers fully backing the cowboy, she had enough complications to wade through. "I'm sure you can find another woman for him to date. He's a good looking man." All the way down to the bare essentials, with all the right equipment—Emma shook herself. "And he's hard-working and considerate."

"But you don't want him." Leslie sighed. "Okay then. I'll see what else I can come up with. I had a hard enough time convincing him to try out my program. I'm not sure he'll give me a second chance."

"If it helps, I'll talk with him the next time I see him."

"Would you?" Leslie's voice lifted. "I have a lot riding on Cooper. If he backs out, I could lose a lot of business."

Emma laughed without feeling much humor. "Way to make me feel even guiltier."

"I'm sorry. I know you did this as a favor, but I've sunk every cent and all the money from Kent's life insurance policy into this business. If I can't get clients to spread the word, I'm sunk."

"What about advertising?"

"I'm counting on word of mouth and individual endorsements. I want strictly handpicked clientele. I've created an exclusive matching making service with a promise of extreme discretion."

"Then why did you want me? I'm just a cowgirl with a degree in animal husbandry."

"Honey, you're a whole lot more than that, and you know it." Leslie snorted. "You've got a masters, you're from a long line of ranchers dating back to when this big ol' state joined the union and you have a heart the size of Texas. I probably would have jumped off a cliff by now if you hadn't joined our support group when you did."

"Good grief, Leslie, you make me sound like a saint, which I'm anything but. Besides, you were well on your way to recovery, and I didn't do anything but say hello."

"You were the friend I needed to kick me in the pants and go after something I'd always wanted to do. Without you encouraging—"

Emma snorted. "Nagging?"

"I never would have done it."

"So it'll be my fault if you lose everything?"

"That's right."

"Back to the original guilt trip."

"Whatever it takes, honey."

"I'll talk to Cooper. Surely, I can persuade him to give you another shot."

"Thanks, Emma. Your effort means the world to me." Leslie paused. "When are you planning to dump Cooper? Officially?"

"Wow, already lining up his next date?"

"I gotta strike while the iron's hot."

"I'll let you know."

"Thanks, Emma. I'm really sorry things didn't work out."

Emma hung up and stared at the phone for a long moment, her heart squeezing.

Leslie was the only person in the world who truly knew what Emma was going through, having lost her husband to cancer. How could she think Emma was ready to jump back into the dating scene? But that was just like Leslie to concentrate on making other people happy to avoid her own sorrow. Setting up the matchmaking service had been an all-consuming task for the young widow, giving her something to focus on besides her loss.

Emma had been her best cheerleader, rooting for her all along the way. What she hadn't considered was Leslie turning her new machine on herself. Reentering the dating scene had never crossed Emma's mind. And to have Cooper selected out of Leslie's limited pool of resources had been unfortunate.

The phone rang again. On reflex, Emma snatched it up. "Hello."

"Emma?"

Emma's pulse rocketed. "Cooper?"

"You sound surprised. You expected my call, didn't you?"

"Yes, yes," she stammered. "Of course. It's all part of the plan."

"Right," he responded, his voice calm and almost cheerful.

Emma's teeth ground together. "What do you want?"

"I thought tonight would be as good as any for our second date? What do you say to an early dinner?"

With a deep, steadying breath, Emma forced air in and out of lungs before responding. "Tonight's not good." Any night wasn't good, as far as going out with Cooper was concerned.

"How about tomorrow night? Unless you want to call it quits now?" He paused.

If Emma told him to buzz off now, her brothers were likely to continue setting her up with more dates. The end of the fake relationship with Cooper had to be a doozy. One that would get her brother's off her back. "No, tomorrow would be better."

"It's your game. Say the word and I flip the switch."

Emma's gut clenched. "I'm sorry, Cooper. This whole situation isn't fair to you. You don't have to play along if you don't want to."

"I've been bored for a while. I find this set of circumstances distracting." He chuckled. "I'll let you know when I'm no longer amused."

"Thanks." She sighed and her fingers tightened on the receiver. "I don't deserve you."

"That's debatable," he parried.

Emma closed her eyes. "I'll see you tomorrow."

Cooper set the phone back in the cradle on the conference room table. "I don't know."

"She agreed to tomorrow night?" Leslie stood on the other side of the table, wringing her hands.

"Yes." Cooper grinned. "Though she didn't sound happy."

Tag stood beside Leslie, a frown pulling his brows

together. "Coop, I have to say this isn't exactly going as I thought it would. You don't have to do this."

Cooper sat back in the leather chair, drumming his fingers on the mahogany surface. "No. I said I'd give Leslie's program a shot."

"Yeah, but from what Leslie was saying, Emma wasn't really committed to finding a match."

"I could look for another match," Leslie offered.

Before Leslie finished the sentence, Cooper was shaking his head. "No. I'm intrigued by the one you found."

Max tapped the table. "But if she's not interested—"

"Then I have to change her mind." Cooper stared around the room at the other three men.

"Are you sure about this?" Gage asked. "If the woman's not willing…"

"We're all successful businessmen." Cooper pushed to his feet. "We put our heads together to make that happen. Surely, we can come up with a way to change Emma's mind."

Leslie crossed her arms, her brow wrinkling. "People aren't businesses, Cooper. Emma's got reasons for not wanting to get involved."

Cooper nodded. "I know about her former fiancé."

"Kind of tough to compete with a memory," Sean pointed out.

"I don't see it that way." Cooper's lips tightened.

Max clapped his hands together. "Well, then, let's help our man find love."

"Now you're talking." Cooper propped his hands on his hips. "What can I do to change her mind?"

"Wine and dine her," Gage suggested.

"She's not a froufrou kind of woman," Cooper countered. "She's all about horses, ranching and the outdoors."

"Sounds like a woman after me own heart." Sean pressed a hand to his chest, emphasizing his Irish accent. "When do we get to meet the lass?"

Hand held upright, Cooper glared. "Back off. Women tend to fall for that smarmy Irish charm."

Leslie sighed. "If you're set on pursuing Emma, you need to learn more about her. Observe her. Find out what she likes and dislikes."

"You mean spy on her?" Sean asked.

"I know a good PI," Max offered.

Gage's brows rose. "Isn't that like stalking?"

"No." Max glared. "It's being aware and informed."

Cooper paced the length of the long table. "I don't want to creep her out or make her hate me. I want her to like me."

"You have to let her get to know you," Leslie said.

"I get one shot at this." Cooper sighed, his hands fisting. "One more date and she'll probably pull the plug on us."

"What's not to like about you, man?" Max stood and draped an arm around his shoulders. "You like ranches, she likes ranches. The match is made in heaven. What more could you ask?"

"More time together. One date isn't going to be enough." Cooper shoved a hand through his hair. "She doesn't leave the ranch often."

"Then you have to be around when she does."

Gage shook his head. "You're back to stalking."

"Talk to her brothers and her friends." Leslie rounded the corner of the table and laid a hand on his arm. "Get to know as much as you can. But don't crowd her. She's still clinging to her fiancé's memory."

"But she's not immune to me." Cooper stared into Leslie's eyes. "I could feel it. Her fiancé might be dead, but she's not."

"Then plan on being where she is when she's there." Max slapped Cooper's back. "Her brothers liked you, work with them. Get their help."

Cooper grinned. "They *did* invite me to watch the Aggies game."

"Like I said, what's not to like about you?" Max grinned.

"Aren't you her friend?" Cooper pinned Leslie with a stare. "What do you know about her?"

Leslie raised her hands. "Sorry, Cooper, you have to work this on your own. If I give you any more information, I run the risk of violating my client's confidentiality."

"Then I better find someone who *can* help me."

Cooper grabbed his cowboy hat and headed for the door.

"Where are you going?"

"To convince my potential future wife she deserves a second chance at love."

"With you?" Max asked.

"Who else?"

CHAPTER 6

"I CAN'T BELIEVE you talked me into coming out to the Ugly Stick tonight." Emma grabbed the long neck bottle of beer from the counter and downed a long slug before she turned to face the saloon's interior.

"You've been holin' up so long you probably forgot how to dance." Ace patted the seat beside him. "Sit, you're as nervous as a cat in a room full of rockin' chairs."

"I'm not in the mood to be out. Too many people are here, it's noisy and smells like tube socks and stale beer."

Brand inhaled deeply and patted his chest. "God, I love that smell. I can feel my chest hairs growin'." He reached out and snagged the waitress as she hurried by. "Charli, honey, could you bring us a pitcher of Guinness?"

Charli raised her brows and stared at the hand on

her arm until Brand let go. "You got it." She spun away, collecting empties as she zigzagged toward the bar.

"That Charli has a lot of sass," Brand noted. "Emma, I think you're right. I need a woman."

Emma rolled her eyes. "Charli's taken."

Brand frowned, his gaze following the pretty waitress. "That's right. Mason's staked his claim, hasn't he?"

"From what I understand, she staked it first," Colton corrected.

"That's what I like...a woman who can take charge." Brand cracked his knuckles. "Well then, who's the lucky girl for this cowboy?"

A chuckle rose up Emma's throat and escaped before she could straighten her lips and give her brother a stern look. "Really, Brand?"

Ace shook his head. "Tone down the ego or you'll never land a decent woman."

"Who said I wanted decent?" He nodded toward a table full of bleach-blondes, wearing short jean skirts and cowboy boots. "Bingo." Brand launched himself from his stool.

Emma grabbed his arm before he got far. "Brand, consider this, those girls have brothers. They're probably some big cowboys' sisters. How would you feel if a heart-breaker like you hit on your sister like you're about to hit on them?"

Brand's chest puffed out for a moment and then

he slumped. "You really know how to take the fun out of a saloon. Did you know that?"

Biting back a smile, Emma turned her brother toward a lone figure at the other end of the bar. "Do yourself a favor and ask that nice young lady to dance."

Brand's smile sank further. "She's not blond."

"Maybe she doesn't have a brother, either." Colton slipped into the seat Brand vacated, a sheen of perspiration glowing across his brow. "Music's hot tonight. Get out there and show Dillon how to two-step. That boy has it all messed up."

Dillon slid onto the stool beside Colton and punched his brother's arm. "I know how to two-step. You were the one crippling your partner, stepping all over her feet."

Emma sighed. Ace had been right. She hadn't been out for a long time and being around her brothers was relaxing as they threw good-natured barbs at each other.

Brand strode to the end of the bar and bowed like a gentleman in front of the quiet brunette.

At first, she shook her head and averted her gaze.

"Ha!" Colton laughed out loud. "She's shootin' him down."

Dillon leaned over Colton's shoulder. "More like crashed and burned."

"Poor girl," Ace said softly. "If only she'd known a

little discouragement is like waving a cape in front of a bull to Brand."

Emma smiled. Brand was the charmer. He could coax a bird out of a tree and a wallflower to bloom with a single smile.

Her brother took the challenge and held out his hand, his mouth parting in a bright, killer smile.

"Doomed," Emma said.

Colton shook his head. "How does he do that?"

"I don't know, but I gotta get me some of that cologne he wears. I swear it's the cologne," Dillon said. The two brothers continued to expound on Brand's technique, their voices fading into the background, music blaring out a boot-scooting song.

"So, what are you going to do about Cooper?" Ace asked.

Jolted back to her own predicament, Emma shot her oldest brother a frown. For a few moments, her siblings' dating life had slipped her own problems to the back of her mind. Now, thanks to Ace, they were back and nagging an ulcer into the pit of her belly. "Why do I have to do anything about Cooper?"

"He's the first guy you haven't kicked out of the house after the first hour."

"That doesn't have to mean anything." Emma lifted her beer, pausing with the rim close to her lips. "Don't read more into it than is there."

"He's a good guy. You could do worse."

"And that's supposed to be an endorsement?"

Instead of taking a drink, she set the bottle on the counter a little harder than she'd intended. "Let this Cooper thing run its course...without interference." She raised her brows, challenging Ace. "If he's still around after a week, so be it."

"And if he's not?"

"You can play the big brother and pick up the pieces of my life." Emma gave him a weak smile. "Like you always have."

"You'll give him a chance?"

Her shoulders rose and lowered. She didn't want to out-and-out lie to her oldest brother, who'd been more like the father she'd lost when she'd been a knob-kneed teen. "I won't tell him to buzz off when he comes to pick me up tomorrow." Her brows narrowed. "But if you continue to throw him at me, I'll...I'll..." She scanned the bar, her thoughts anywhere but there. "I'll move."

"What, out of the house?" Ace's mouth gaped.

She shook her head. "No. Out of the state." Her gaze returned to Ace, her jaw tight. "I had an offer to train horses in New Hampshire. If you keep pushing me the way you have, I might just take them up on it."

"You hate snow."

"I hate being railroaded by my brothers more than I hate snow."

Ace glared. "You wouldn't go. You love Texas too much."

Her brows rose higher. "As you put it, I need to move on."

The oldest Jacobs sibling raised his hands. "Okay, okay. I'll back off. But you have to promise me, you'll pull yourself out of the funk you've been in for the past two years."

Emma nodded. "Agreed." She glanced around. "Now, I need to find the ladies room."

"I'll hold your seat for you." Ace laid his cowboy hat on the barstool she'd never sat on.

If she was crafty, she'd take the opportunity to ditch her brothers and return home. She had the keys to Ace's truck. Brand had driven his own truck with the intention of spending the night with some lucky lady. He could give the others a ride home, if need be.

With a half-formed plan in mind, Emma headed for the powder room.

COOPER PUSHED through the entrance of the Ugly Stick Saloon, the music hitting him like a two-ton bull square in the chest. A lively polka had dancers up and gyrating on the worn wooden floor. People were laughing, hugging, smiling and happy. He found it hard not to get caught up in the mood. But he wasn't there to go with the flow. Cooper was on a mission.

Earlier, he'd called Ace to ask when they could get together. He'd made up a lame excuse about wanting to know how to deal with a colicky horse. Not that any of his horses had colic, but the ruse gave him a reason to see Emma's oldest brother. After his meeting with the BAs and Leslie from the Billionaire Online Dating Service, Cooper was even more determined to bring Emma over to the idea of dating again. Even if a relationship didn't work out between them, he had to have the opportunity to find out.

The woman was far too interesting to let slip away. She was gutsy, strong and wasn't afraid to speak up for what she wanted. Cooper supposed growing up among her brothers had forced her to be that way or get lost among the burly cowboys.

Ace waved from across the room. He sat with Colton and Dillon at the bar.

Cooper glanced around for Brand and Emma, breathing a relieved sigh when he didn't find Emma.

Brand led a pretty brunette toward the dance floor.

Cooper had hoped to get Ace alone for a little one-on-one prying into Emma's life. Of all the brothers, Ace was the oldest and probably the most discreet. And like the rest, he cared about his little sister.

The band struck up a lively rendition of the Cotton-Eyed Joe. Colton and Dillon bolted from their seats, plucked two women from their chairs and joined the growing throng on the dance floor. Cooper heaved a sigh. Good. One Jacobs brother was enough to handle when he had work to do.

"Name your poison," Ace said as Cooper slid into the seat vacated by Colton.

"Bud."

Ace waved to the female bartender. "Libby, get my friend a Bud."

"On tap or bottle?" she asked.

"Tap," Cooper replied.

Libby tugged the tap, filling a mug with clear golden brew.

Cooper didn't speak until he had his fist curled around the frosted glass. "Thanks for meeting with me."

"Colicky filly, huh?" Ace's mouth twisted then curled up on the corners. "Right."

Heat rose up Cooper's neck and he shifted on his stool. "Okay, so I'm more interested in a different kind of filly."

Ace glanced over Cooper's shoulder before he continued. "Look, the filly in question is here tonight. I think she might bolt for the door, so we don't have much time."

Cooper's head jerked up and he panned the bar for Emma's tall, lithe form. "I'm listening."

"We like you, Cooper. If we didn't, you and I wouldn't be having this conversation."

"Good to know."

"Emma's stuck on her dead fiancé...no...more clinging to his memory." Ace's brows drew together. "I think she's afraid of letting go."

Cooper's chest tightened. "Why?"

"She really did love him and there might be some guilt for wanting a life after all he sacrificed." He shrugged. "I can only guess."

"She wants me to dump her after our first real date." Cooper stared into his beer.

"She said that?" Ace shook his head. "Damn fool." He grinned. "Consider yourself lucky."

His brows rising, Cooper glanced up. "Lucky?"

"Most men we bring home don't get past *hello*." Ace crossed his arms. "How interested are you?"

Cooper shrugged and took a drink before he answered. "Too soon to ask her to marry me, but I do know she's special."

"Go on."

"She's smart, pretty, loves horses and she's sexy."

Ace closed his eyes for a moment then opened them. "I didn't need to hear that last part."

"Well, she is." Cooper sat straighter. "And she's honest, loyal to her family and has a great capacity for love which is obvious in her feelings toward her brothers."

Ace nodded. "Okay, you're saying all the right things. What are you going to do?"

"I want to know more about her. Her likes, dislikes, what makes her happy, her favorite food, what she likes on her pizza."

Ace frowned. "You're starting to sound like a stalker."

"If I'm going to win her over, I have to know what makes her tick."

"Granted." Ace looked past Cooper. "She threatened to leave if I kept pushing you at her. To move to another state. So whatever I tell you, don't come on too strong, or she'll know someone put you up to it."

"Understood." Cooper's heart skipped a couple beats at the thought of Emma moving out of state. Was he interested enough to follow her? God, if he did, she'd have a restraining order put out against him. He'd have to win her over before she flew the coop.

"She likes action movies, hates what she calls girlie romantic comedies. Likes dogs more than cats, pepperoni on her pizza and light beer, not wine."

Cooper committed Ace's confidences to memory. "What about dates? Where would she prefer to go?"

"She's not much into ritzy dining. Would rather go to a barbeque joint than a five-star restaurant. Hell, there she goes." He jerked his chin toward the rear of the saloon. "If you want to see her tonight, you better catch her now."

Cooper's head whipped around.

Emma hugged the wall, staying in the shadows, making her way toward the exit. She cast a glance toward the bar where Ace and Cooper sat.

Cooper ducked his head. He didn't want her to know he'd been chatting with her brother. She wouldn't be too happy they'd been discussing her.

When she reached the front door, she cast one last glance their way then slipped out.

"Does she like to dance?" Cooper asked as he stood, plunking his cowboy hat on his head.

"Yes, but she hasn't since Marcus died. And she prefers the waltz to two-stepping. Or at least she did with Marcus." Ace patted his back, giving him a little shove. "Go. She'll be taking my truck since she road with me. It's a black four-by-four parked beneath the lamp post near the rear. You can beat her to it, if you go out the back."

"Thanks." Cooper wove through the crowd, slipped behind the bar and through the doorway leading to the back of the saloon.

A large women, dressed in black jeans, a black shirt and a stern expression stepped in his path. "This area is off limits."

Cooper ground to a halt, stopping short of plowing into the battleaxe. "I need to get to my girl before she leaves." He made a move to go around the woman.

She blocked him. "Sorry. You'll have to leave through the front door."

The big woman refused to budge, and short of manhandling her, Cooper had to follow her advice.

"Greta Sue, it's okay, let the man pass."

Cooper spun to face a pretty, petite strawberry-blonde.

The younger woman smiled and waved the

bouncer aside. "Ace says you're in a hurry to catch his sister. Don't let us stand in the way of love."

Cooper tipped his hat. "Thanks. I owe you." He frowned as he stepped past Greta Sue. "By the way, who are you?" he asked as he sprinted for the exit.

"Audrey Anderson," she called out. "I own the Ugly Stick Saloon."

"Thanks again, ma'am." He pushed through the back door and out into the gravel parking lot, making a note to himself to return and thank the woman properly.

Not until he found the truck beneath the lamp post did Audrey's uttered words hit him. *She didn't want to stand in the way of love...*

Cooper stood for a moment, digesting the meaning. Love? Him? Hell, he'd only met the woman once. Love was something you grew into. Or at least, that's what he'd been told. He'd yet to fall in love, and the foster homes he'd lived in hadn't shown him a single example of what love should be. The only reference he had was the kind of love he'd seen in movies. Based on the tabloids, even movie stars fell in and out of love in the length of time a cold took to run its course.

What was he doing, standing outside in the dark...okay under a dingy yellow light...waiting for a woman who loved a dead man? He was supposed to be a smart man. If he wasn't, he wouldn't be a billionaire. Then why was he mooning over a woman he couldn't have?

Was he compelled because he couldn't have her? Everything else came easy to him lately, now that he had money. Women who knew he was rich threw themselves at him. He could have any one of them without going to all this effort.

Could the truth be that he liked the challenge of Emma Jacobs? What would happen when he captured her attention, maybe even her love? Would he grow bored and leave her?

Holy hell. What was he thinking? All these thoughts took only seconds to whip through his brain. He stepped out, ready to go back to the bar or leave.

A woman, not Emma, rounded the corner of the building. Or rather staggered around the corner and fell to her knees.

"Ruth, wait." Emma emerged immediately behind her. "You're too drunk. You can't drive."

"Have to get away." The woman named Ruth sat back on her haunches, her head hanging down, hair covering her face. "That jerk."

"Honey, let me help you." Emma soothed her with a hand stroking her back while the other hooked the woman's arm and tried to lift her. Her voice was soft, gentle, caring.

Cooper's heart swelled. Emma was one of those

women who'd do anything for a friend, even take her car keys to keep her from doing something stupid.

"No." Ruth shoved Emma's hands away. "I got this." She staggered to her feet, dug in her pocket for her keys and half-walked, half-fell toward a tiny, bright red Mazda Miata with a rag top.

Emma chased after Ruth and snatched the keys from her hand. "I'm not letting you drive like this."

Cooper stepped away from Ace's truck. "Need a hand?"

Emma jumped and spun to face him, dropping into a ready stance.

Cooper suspected she was ready to kick butt to protect herself and her friend. He grinned and raised his hands. "Sorry, didn't mean to scare you. You look like you could use a hand."

"Don't need a man," Ruth slurred and fell against the car. "Nothin' but trouble..." The woman's eyes rolled to the back of her head and she slid toward the ground.

Before Emma could catch Ruth, Cooper leaped forward and scooped her up. The alcohol on her breath made him reel. "She's not driving."

"I can take her home," Emma said.

"No." Ruth's head lolled. "Call my brother."

Emma touched a hand to the woman's cheek. "It's not a problem, really."

"Brother." Ruth passed out again.

Emma shrugged, tugged her cell phone from her

purse and scrolled through her contact list before punching one. She pressed the phone to her ear and stared at Cooper over the inert drunk woman. "Pete? Emma Jacobs. Ruth asked me to call you. Yeah, she's sort of okay. She needs a ride home from the Ugly Stick. Yeah, a little too much. Five minutes? Great. We'll be waiting in the back parking lot."

Emma's gaze never left Cooper's as she spoke to Pete on the phone.

The heat her gaze generated made holding a drunk well worth the effort.

When she hung up, Emma tipped her head sideways. "When Pete gets here, we need to talk."

Cooper tipped his head.

He could tell she wasn't happy about seeing him. But something about the way Emma carried herself —self-assured, determined, yet vulnerable—made Cooper keep coming back. Maybe he had some masochistic tendencies, given the pain of her consistent rejection. Perhaps he saw something behind the wall she'd erected around her heart.

All he knew was he had to find a way through that wall. He suspected that beneath the rubble piled over her heart, he'd find a treasure. Cooper hoped she'd give him enough time to mine for the truth.

CHAPTER 7

FIVE MINUTES OF SEMI-SILENCE, laced with the thrum of muted music radiating through the walls of the saloon, and with Ruth's occasional rise to consciousness and incoherent slurs slid by like molasses in the winter.

The entire time Emma alternated between anger at Cooper's appearance and a strange joy she found more disturbing than she could have imagined.

Pete pulled up in a rusty pickup and settled his sister in the front seat. "Thanks, Emma."

Emma sighed. "She'd do the same for me."

Pete shook his head. "I don't think I've ever seen you that drunk. Ever." He hugged Emma. "Thanks for keeping Ruth off the road."

When the truck pulled away, Emma chose anger over joy and faced Cooper, hands jammed on her hips. "What the hell are you doing here?"

Cooper grinned. "Nice to see you, too."

Guilt forced Emma to soften her voice. "Sorry. I wasn't expecting to see you tonight."

"I know."

"So, why are you here? Don't you live in Dallas?"

"I have a place not far from here. Felt like having a beer, so I dropped in."

"Just happened to drop in?" Her eyes narrowed as she stared at Cooper. She didn't believe him. Had he come to see her? Butterflies stirred the beer in her gut. "Funny, I've never seen you at the Ugly Stick."

"Probably because most of my business keeps me busy and running to Dallas. I haven't taken much time to go out lately. Something I vow to change."

Emma rummaged in her pockets for the keys. "Well, I hope you enjoy it. I'm headed home."

"Look, since you're here, do you think you could spare a single dance?"

Her heart fluttered, heat pooled low in her belly, and her breath came in tight, shallow pants. "No." She hadn't danced with a man since Marcus left for the war. "No."

"It's been a long time since I've done a two-step. If I'm to give Leslie's program another shot, I could use a few lessons." He smiled, an eyebrow lifted. "I promise not to step on your toes too often."

The reference to Leslie did the trick. "You do realize you're using emotional blackmail, don't you?"

Cooper's grin broadened. "Yes, ma'am. Whatever

it takes. I have two left feet and I couldn't possibly jump back into the dating scene without a little help."

Emma hesitated. Her mind told her to run as fast as she could, but her body leaned toward Cooper. An errant thought pushing its way into her subconscious. What would it be like to be held by the tall dark cowboy? To have his arms close around her and guide her to the rhythm of the music? A long time had passed since she'd had a man's arms around her...arms that didn't belong to one of her brothers.

"Just one dance. That's all I'm asking. Then we can both go our separate ways." He lifted her hand, his fingers closing around hers, sending electric shocks skittering along her nerve endings. "Please."

She snatched away her hand. Emma's head told her this was a bad idea. But when she opened her mouth... "Fine. But only one. Then I'm headed home to bed."

As soon as the last word left her mouth, she could have bit off her tongue. The mention of bed led to more lusty thoughts than she'd intended.

"Shall we go back in?" Cooper waved one hand toward the saloon.

Emma didn't want to face her brothers. They'd consider the night a success if she danced with Cooper in front of them. And she didn't want to add to their disappointment when she left Cooper behind. "No, the music is loud enough we can do it out here."

Cooper's lips curved upward. His fingers tightened around hers and he drew her into his arms.

Emma held back, keeping a distance of six inches between them, afraid of her body's reaction. Lust was a natural instinct, one that could spike as skin touched skin and music stirred the soul. The emotion didn't replace love, she reminded herself—the love she'd shared with Marcus.

But the heat sure muddied the waters.

"You've done the two-step before, right?" She stared up into Cooper's eyes. Another mistake. He tipped his head, allowing the light from overhead to shine beneath the rim of his cowboy hat and into his face, making the blue of his irises sparkle like diamonds.

Emma caught her breath.

"I did the two-step back in my college party days, but I'm pretty rusty." The muscles of his shoulders bunched beneath Emma's palm as his hand slipped down low on her waist, his fingers warm and firm.

"It's easy," Emma squeaked, finding breathing hard with Cooper's hand heating her back and other areas farther south. "You start out on your left foot with a step-together, then a full step and another step."

"Like this?" His grip tightened and he stepped out with a quickstep.

Emma moved with him easily, the pattern simple and easy to follow with the music thrumming through the tin walls of the Ugly Stick. "Yes. That's it."

They moved around the gravel parking lot, swaying to the beat, perfectly synchronized as if they'd danced together for a lifetime.

The moon shone full and bright, stars twinkled from the heavens and a soft late summer breeze lifted the hair off the back of Emma's neck.

For a moment, she could pretend they were alone in the world, only the two of them. No brothers interfering, no past, no future, no expectations, just the present and a single dance. Emma relaxed and let the music and Cooper's lead carry her.

As the song ended, another started—this one slow, sensuous, a song meant for belt-buckle-polishing closeness. Without missing a step, Cooper pulled Emma closer.

She melted against him, her cheek resting against his chest. The scent of soap, aftershave and male wafted through her senses as the hard ridge beneath his fly pressed into her belly.

Molten heat roiled through her body, and as if of their own volition, her hands rose to circle behind Cooper's neck.

Both of his claimed her lower back, nudging her even tighter against him as the muffled music droned on. They swayed slower and slower until they came to a standstill.

The music flowed on around them, but Emma couldn't move. Her gaze rose to the sparkling blue of Cooper's, reflecting the starlight.

His mouth came down over hers, gentle at first, then with increasing pressure, his tongue pushing past her lips and teeth to stroke the length of hers.

Emma's fingers laced through Cooper's dark hair, knocking the hat from his head.

Something about exposing the cowboy's head to the moonlight made Emma's nipples tight and rub deliciously against the lace of her bra, a leg circling behind Cooper's.

"Hey, get a room," a man called out.

Emma pushed away from Cooper, her eyes wide, her heart hammering against her ribs. "That shouldn't have happened."

Cooper reached out with both arms. "But it did."

Her head shaking back and forth, Emma pressed a fist to her lips. "No. It can't. I love Marcus."

Cooper's jaw tightened and his arms fell to his sides. "Emma, Marcus is gone."

With pain radiating through her chest, Emma pressed a hand against her breast to ease it. "I have to go." She spun and ran for Ace's pickup. Once inside, she blindly jabbed the key into the ignition. She took three tries to get it in. Then she yanked the gear into reverse and spun out of the parking lot.

Despite her determination not to, Emma glanced in her rearview mirror.

Cooper scooped his hat off the ground and stood in the glow of the overhead light, watching her. Then he ran his hand through his hair.

Emma's fingers tingled with the remembered texture of that hair. She forced her focus on the road, her hands tightening around the steering wheel, the night blurring past as she sped home.

Once inside the ranch house, she raced for her room and dragged a box from beneath the bed. One by one, she pulled out pictures, keepsakes and articles of clothing. All belonging to Marcus and their life together. Nelson trotted into the room and lay down beside her, his golden chin resting on her thigh.

"Why is this happening?" Emma stroked the dog's head. "I loved Marcus. There's no other man I want in my life."

Nelson whined and nudged her hand when it stopped the stroking motion.

Emma lifted Marcus's dog tags from the bottom of the box and held the chain in her fingers. Tears slipped from the corners of her eyes.

"Why did you leave me?" More tears followed the first. Emma stared at the picture on her nightstand of Marcus and her. When she closed her eyes, the image faded, replaced by Cooper standing in the moonlight after a kiss that should never have happened.

Emma clutched Marcus's dog tags to her chest and curled up beside the golden retriever on the braided rug. "Why did you leave me?" she whispered.

As exhaustion claimed Emma, Marcus's voice seemed to whisper through the open window, "I never did and never will."

COOPER DROVE HOME that night his thoughts in more of a turmoil than when he'd set out earlier that evening. When he walked through the door of his ranch house, the phone rang.

He ignored the first ring. Then he thought, what if the caller was Emma? He snatched the device from the cradle and slammed it against his ear. "Hello."

"Coop, the suspense is killing me. What have you found out?"

"Tag?" Cooper glanced at his watch. "Do you know how late it is?"

"Past midnight. I couldn't sleep."

"What if *I'd* been asleep?"

"With a woman on your mind?" His friend snorted. "Right. Stop stalling. What did you find out?"

Cooper jerked his hat off his head and tossed it on the table beside the phone base. "Her brother Ace managed to get her to go out tonight to the Ugly Stick Saloon outside Temptation. I just happened to be there."

Tag whooped. "Way to go. The more she sees you, the more she's likely to fall for you, man."

"I'm not so sure." Remembering the stricken look on her face, Cooper raked his fingers through his hair. "She's really hung up on her late fiancé."

"He's out of the picture."

"Yeah, but if she does go for me, will I be her rebound?"

Tag sighed. "Hmmm. You have a point. What you have to decide is if she's worth the risk."

Exactly what Cooper had been thinking. Visions of Emma staring up at him in the moonlight and the tingle of warmth still emanating through him from her body pressed close as they'd danced and then kissed... "Man, I think she's the one for me. The question is if I'm the one for her. I don't think she's ready to move forward."

"Have you kissed her?"

Cooper hesitated, his own cowboy code kicking in. A man didn't kiss and tell.

"You did," Tag responded for him. "And?"

His lips tingled. He could still taste Emma. "None of your business."

"Must have been good if you're not sharing." Tag chuckled. "I'm guessing she kissed you back. Otherwise, you wouldn't have your chaps in a twist."

Cooper shook his head, a smile tugging at his lips. "Anyone ever tell you that you're annoying?"

"All the time. Part of my charm."

"So you called to torment me?"

"Just following up to see if you made any progress today. Did you learn anything more about her likes and dislikes?"

"Ace gave me a few pointers."

"Good. Tomorrow, you have to put them all to

work. Oh, and since you didn't want to hire a private investigator to look into your Emma's background, I did."

Cooper was already shaking his head. "I didn't hear that. I wouldn't violate her privacy any more than I have by asking her brothers about her. I felt bad enough as it was."

"Hmm, then I guess you don't want to know she's planning to buy a spread of her own."

That got his attention. As a man who'd only recently purchased his own three-thousand acre ranch to plant some roots, Cooper was keenly interested in land deals and sales. But then, this was Emma. "She lives on her family's ranch. Why would she want to buy her own?"

"Got your interest, did it?"

Cooper shook his head. "Never mind. I don't want to know."

"If you do. I can tell you where it is and how much the owner is asking."

"If Emma and I make it as a couple, I want it to be based on truth and honesty. I want her to be with me because she loves me. Not because I can buy her anything her heart desires."

"What good is money if you can't spoil the people you care about?"

Cooper could only shake his head at Tag's attitude. "Not everyone wants to be spoiled."

"My point exactly. Apparently, your Emma has

been saving her money to buy this piece, refusing to let her brothers buy it for her."

Emma rose another notch in Cooper's estimation. The woman had enough spunk and gumption for two. "Please don't investigate further."

"Doesn't hurt to know as much as possible about the woman. Gets you past the awkward silences of getting to know each other. Speaking of which...good luck tomorrow on your first real date together."

If Emma didn't cancel on him between now and the following evening. "I gotta get some rest."

"Yeah, you want to be in top form when you sweep the future Mrs. Johnson off her feet."

"Hey. I'm taking her out, not asking her to marry me. I've only known Emma for a day and a half."

"You've heard of love at first sight, haven't you?"

"I don't buy into all that crap."

"Time will tell."

"Goodnight, Tag."

"'Night."

Cooper hung up, more disturbed than when he'd walked through his front door.

Love at first sight?

Nah.

That experience couldn't happen to a man who grew up in the foster system. He didn't believe in love at first sight or happily-ever-afters. The concepts didn't exist.

Or did they?

He strode through house, viewing it with a fresh eye. The single-story home had been tastefully decorated in Southwest ranch style with floor-to-ceiling windows in most rooms and raised ceilings. Completely furnished, the place was his retreat from the hustle of Dallas and the constant motion and churning of traffic and humans.

At the ranch, he had everything he needed to be self-sufficient. He'd worked hard over the past ten years to accumulate enough wealth to never again be dependent on anyone. The foster homes had taught him that much.

Still, the house felt empty...incomplete.

Cooper kicked off his boots and stripped out of his jeans and shirt. Emma's scent clung to his skin as he lay across the king-size bed in the master bedroom. The hum of cicadas drifted in through his open window, making the room feel bigger, like he was sleeping in the vastness of the outdoors.

Alone.

He wanted to rail against Leslie and her damned match-making program. Before he'd met Emma, he'd thought he had everything.

Emma and the Jacobs brothers brought the fact home that he didn't.

Hell, he didn't have anything that counted.

To the Jacobs, things could be replaced, family was forever.

Not for the first time in his life, Cooper wished for a family.

CHAPTER 8

DAWN HAD YET to come when Emma woke to Nelson's tongue scraping across her cheek. She turned away her face, a crick in her neck causing her to flinch. "Get off the bed," she muttered.

Nelson licked her again and jumped to his feet, toenails clicking across wooden floors.

Emma opened her eyes, the gray haze of pre-dawn illuminating the fact she'd slept on the floor. Photos and memorabilia scattered as she sat up. The dog tags she'd gone to sleep clutching jangled against her fingers.

She pressed a kiss to the cold hard metal and pushed to a standing position. With a sigh, she carefully placed all the items back in the box and closed the lid, feeling for the first time like she was closing the box containing her old life. Frowning, she lifted the cardboard container and hiked it up onto the shelf in her closet, next to her high school scrapbook and an old doll her mother had given her when she was six.

What made her move the box from beneath her bed to her closet, Emma didn't know. She just felt the time was right, and that thought made her sad. After closing the closet door, she entered the bathroom, brushed her teeth, pulled her hair back in a low ponytail and slipped out of the clothes she'd been wearing the night before, when Cooper had kissed her.

Another glance in the mirror proved she was still Emma. The same woman who'd gone to the bar last night had come back unchanged in physical appearance. But inside a nervous, restless twitchiness forced her out of the bathroom and back into her bedroom where she flung on clean jeans, boots and an old T-shirt.

Before the sun came up, Emma was in the barn, mucking stalls and feeding horses. As the golden orb peeked over the horizon, she sat astride her palomino mare, riding across the pasture, away from the house and the prying eyes and minds of her well-meaning brothers. She had a lot to do today. A gate needed mending, a fence on the north forty needed to be restretched and the pasture near the creek needed mowing. But for now, she rode hard, letting Daisy have her head, the cool morning air giving them both the lift and vibrancy they needed to face the day.

When she returned to the house, she ducked into the kitchen. Her brothers had yet to make an appearance. Probably stayed out too late at the Ugly Stick. Maybe nursing hangovers. Just as well.

Emma couldn't face the inquisition. Not yet. Not after the kiss that had rocked her world and awakened desires she thought had died with Marcus.

Working quietly, she slapped together a quick sandwich out of leftover ham, grabbed her hat and slipped back outside.

A working ranch with over two thousand head of cattle and a herd of thirty horses, the Rockin' J Ranch bred Angus cattle and trained both thoroughbred and quarter horses. With several hired hands. Emma didn't have to lift a finger and the work got done. That wasn't her style. Emma pitched in on the evenings and weekends when she wasn't working at the T-Bar-M Ranch.

She'd never let her family's money influence her behavior, preferring the hard work of a rancher, over that of a pampered princess. With money, employees and animals, came responsibility. Emma dreamed of the day when she could afford a house of her own, built with the money she'd earned. Oh sure, she could have taken money from the family coffers, and built a home worthy of the Southern Living magazine by now, but doing so wouldn't have felt like she'd earned it. Now she had almost enough to buy the little one-hundred and fifty-acre farm down by Willow Creek. Old Man Rausch said he'd let her know if someone showed interest in the property before he sold it, to give her a chance to make an offer first.

She planned to meet with him by the end of the week and start the paperwork. Soon, she'd be the owner of her own place, free and clear of her brothers and her family's wealth. Only then would she feel like she could make her own way.

Marcus had been less than enthusiastic about the Willow Creek place. He'd argued that when they married, she'd follow him around from post to post, finding work wherever she could.

Young and in love, Emma would have done anything to please Marcus and she would have been happy doing it, as long as she was with him. Now that she was so close to owning her own place, she looked forward to rolling up her sleeves and making it her own.

Too bad, she wouldn't have anyone to share it with.

As soon as that thought surfaced, another followed with an image of Cooper tossing hay bales onto the back of a trailer, shirtless and coated in a shiny layer of sweat.

The heat of the sun had nothing to do with the flames bursting inside Emma. She grabbed the post-hole diggers and tossed them into the back of the work truck, then loaded several wood posts and a come-along and wire cutters. She was headed for the stack of T-posts when Jared Kramer, the youngest of the ranch hands, trotted up alongside her.

"Let me get those, Miss Emma."

"I can do it," she said, reaching for three posts.

"I know you can, but I feel better if I do it for you." Jared smiled. "My mamma taught me to be a gentleman."

Emma grinned. "She did a good job."

The eighteen-year-old grabbed a bundle of ten, flung it up on his shoulder like the load was nothing and carried it to the back of the waiting truck. He returned to the barn for a roll of field fence, then again for a roll of barbed wire, while Emma searched for twist ties, fence staples and a hammer.

Jared grabbed the chainsaw, a jug of gas and a file and tossed them in with the fencing supplies. "That ought to do it. Reckon you'll need a hand with that fence." The teen hooked his thumbs in his belt loops and rocked back on his dusty dingo boots. "Are you driving or am I?"

Emma frowned. She'd wanted to mend the fence to have time by herself to think through what was happening in her life and what she wanted to do about it. But the job wasn't a one-man or one-woman job. "I'll drive."

Jared climbed into the passenger seat and sat in silence throughout the fifteen-minute drive to the far corner of the property. Without being told, he climbed down from the truck and opened gates, closing them behind the truck when she'd gone through.

They spent the day, cutting the downed tree, removing the old fence and snapped posts and digging holes and setting the new poles. Once all the posts were in place, Emma hooked the come-along to the fence puller. While Jared held the field fence off the ground, she cranked the wench until the wire stretched taut.

Jared grabbed the hammer and a pocket full of fence staples and tacked the fence to a wooden pole.

Emma twist-tied the wire to the steel posts in between the wooden posts. When the fence was secure, she let off the tension on the come-along and the fence stood straight and tight, with shiny new wire.

The sun dipped toward the horizon as Jared and Emma loaded the truck with the old fence and the supplies and headed back to the barn.

A four-wheeler met them halfway back. Brand pulled up beside the truck, a frown marring his brow. "Do you realize how late it is?"

"No." Emma frowned. "The clock on the truck doesn't work."

"You have exactly twenty minutes to get ready for your date."

Emma's gut clenched. Working alongside the

quiet, yet efficient, Jared all day long, she'd let the strain of her muscles push the stress of her life to the side. Now, thanks to Brand's reminder, the worries all came rushing back like a tsunami on the beach, undermining her confidence. "I'll call and cancel."

"You can't. He will have left his house by now. You know, cell phone reception is spotty between towns. "

"Damn. I still have to unload the truck."

"Here, take the four-wheeler." Brand climbed off the ATV, opened the door to the truck. "Jared and I can unload the truck. You need a shower, you smell."

"Love you too, brother." With Brand waiting and twenty minutes to repair the damage of a day's work in the field, Emma didn't have time to waste. She hopped on the back of the four-wheeler.

"And do something nice with your hair," Brand called out. "Don't worry about the gates. We'll close them."

Emma raced ahead of the truck, blowing through the gates Brand had left open on his ride out to get her. When she reached the ranch house, she skidded to a stop in the gravel and jumped off.

Ace, Colton and Dillon leaped off the porch.

"Holy hell, Emma, you're a wreck." Ace gripped her elbow and hurried her toward the house.

Dillon hooked her other arm and between the two of them, they practically carried her up the steps to the porch.

"Put me down. I've been working all day, which is more than I can say for you all."

"We've been working. But you're the one with the date. You better get moving, or you'll be in your altogether when he gets here."

Colton grabbed for the screen door and held it open, waggling his eyebrows. "Unless that was the plan all along. Maybe move this relationship along a little faster that way."

Emma punched his arm as she crossed the threshold, glaring. "Enough. You're my brothers, for crissakes. You're supposed to pummel his ass for even thinking of me naked."

"Grow up, little sis." Dillon shook his head. "We're all adults here." He marched her down the hallway and shoved her through her bathroom door. "Get in there and scrub the horse manure off at the very least. Sheesh."

Ace and Colton stood in her doorway, laughing.

With all the anger she could muster in her tired body, Emma slammed shut the door between them. "Brothers! Who needs enemies when you have family to railroad your life?" Despite her ire, she flipped on the shower and stripped her dirty cloths, stirring up a mist of Texas dust floating in the air.

When she stepped into the shower, the cool water washed the rest of the dust down her body in muddy rivulets, pooling at her feet. No wonder they'd been upset. She could plant a garden in the amount of dirt she'd acquired on her skin during the long, hot day.

With a heaping dollop of herbal shampoo, she scrubbed the sweat and dirt from her hair and face. Then with a washcloth, she attacked her body, leaving it glowing pink and clean and a dark ring of dirt clinging to the tub.

With a sigh, she shut off the water and stepped out of the shower, wrapping her hair turban-style in a clean, dry towel and another twisted around her body. Careful not to step into the dust around her discarded clothing, Emma made quick work of brushing the tangles from her hair, hitting it with a blow dryer until it lay in soft waves around her shoulders. A quick wand of mascara on her lashes and she was done. The sun had done the job of making her cheeks pink and her skin glowed.

Pounding on her bedroom door made her jump.

"He's driving up. Are you about ready?"

"Hell no," she yelled. "But I will be."

Emma raced through her bedroom to her closet and flung open the door, her gaze skimming across the array of blouses and jeans and landing on a pale yellow sundress she'd purchased a month ago and never worn. She hadn't felt like dressing up or going out for so long, she didn't know why she'd bought it in the first place. But the garment had been hanging in the window of a little store on Main Street in Temptation. When she'd walked by, the dress caught her attention and she'd bought it without thinking too hard.

With no time to spare, she grabbed it off the hanger, dropped her towel, clipped on a bra, slipped the dress over her head and her feet into lacy panties and then a pair of simple sandals.

"There. Not too dressy and not too fancy. It'll have to do for our last date." The wind blew out of her sails as she stepped out of her bedroom. Tonight would be the last time she saw Cooper.

"Coop, how's it going?" Ace's voice carried down the hallway from the front porch.

Emma sucked in a deep breath and hurried to the door.

When she stepped out into the bright sunshine, she blinked twice before she could focus on Cooper.

He wore dark slacks, a crisply pressed white, long-sleeved shirt and a red tie. In his hands, he carried a loose bunch of daisies. And his smile made Emma's knees wobble.

His eyes widened and his gaze traveled from the tip of her head to her sandals. "Wow. You look incredible."

The butterflies in her stomach rose in a flutter. "You're not bad, for a desk jockey."

He executed a half-bow.

"You look a lot better than you did fifteen minutes ago." Ace pressed a kiss to Emma's forehead. "The girl can clean up."

"Are those for me?" she asked, indicating the flowers.

"Well, if not for you, I'm not taking them." Brand laughed. "Seriously, sis. You weren't born yesterday."

Emma's lips twitched. "Shut up, Brand."

Cooper handed her the daisies. "I went to pick up roses, but when I saw these, they reminded me of you."

Emma took the flowers and held them close, struggling to breathe past the lump in her throat.

Marcus had always given her red roses. Now that he was gone, they reminded her more of death than of love.

"I hope you don't mind the daisies."

"They're perfect." She stared down at the flowers, fighting to keep tears from falling. "I'll just put these in water." Before he could stop her, Emma spun and hurried back into the house, headed for the kitchen where she stopped in front of the sink, clutching the flowers like a lifeline. Footsteps behind her let her know she wasn't alone.

"You okay?" Dillon reached up beside her and retrieved a Mason jar, filled it with water and set it on the counter.

"Yeah, sure. Why wouldn't I be?"

"I don't know. Your face looked like it does when you're about to cry." Dillon took the flowers from her hands and arranged them in the water-filled jar. "You don't have to go out with him if you don't want to."

Emma swiped at an errant tear sliding down her cheek. "No. It's okay. I just thought the daisies were sweet."

Dillon gripped her arms and forced her to face him. "You still miss Marcus that much?"

She leaned into her brother's chest, shaking her head. "That's just it. I don't."

He set her away and frowned down. "I don't get it. If you're not missing Marcus, what's the problem?"

"Marcus was so much a part of my life, even after he died, not having him to cling to scares the crap out of me."

Dillon scraped the next tear from her cheek. "You'll be okay."

"How do you know?"

"Because you're one of us. Jacobs don't crack under pressure. We rise like cream to the top." He grinned. "Now, smile and get out there. Cooper's a good guy. But if he's not the one for you, that's okay too. Just do us a favor, will ya?"

Emma sniffed and forced a smile. "What's that?"

"Don't crawl back into your shell. You're too pretty to be hiding." He kissed her forehead, spun her around and smacked her butt. "Now go get 'em."

Emma walked slowly through the house, her steps lightening as she went. Her brothers were right. She needed to get on with her life. Marcus would have wanted her to.

But damn, the idea was scary.

Cooper leaned against a post on the porch, a lock of his dark hair hanging over his forehead. He laughed at something Colton was saying, the sparkle in his eye still evident as Emma stepped out.

Her breath caught and held as she wavered on the doorstep.

"Ready?" He held out his hand.

Emma stared at it a moment, sucked in a deep breath and took it. "I'm ready."

"Y'all have a great time." Ace clapped Cooper on the back, then squeezed the man's shoulder. "But not too good a time. I'd hate to ride shotgun to your wedding."

Heat blossomed in Emma's cheeks. "Ace."

Her oldest brother held up his hands. "Just sayin'."

"Don't listen to him," Brand said. "He's all stuffy and full of himself, thinkin' he has to play daddy and polish his guns. Just have fun and don't do anything I wouldn't." Brand winked and chucked her beneath her chin.

Ace glared. "Which doesn't leave out anything."

"Exactly." Brand caught Emma's hand with one of his own, while fishing in his pocket with the other. He pulled out a dark foil packet and slapped it into her palm. "Just be careful."

"Brand!" Her face hot to the tips of her ears, Emma ducked her head. "I can't believe you did that." She curled her hand around the packet and shoved it into her sundress pocket. "Let's go." With her other hand still in Cooper's, she led the way down the steps and half-dragged the man to his truck.

He held the door open, a smile tugging at his lips.

Emma's lips pressed together. "Don't say a thing."

Cooper's eyes widened. "I wouldn't dare."

COOPER DIDN'T MENTION Brand's gift, but he couldn't have wiped the grin off his face if he'd had a gun pressed to his temple. He backed out, swung around and headed down the long drive and through the arched gate of the Rockin' J Ranch. "I thought we'd head into Dallas for dinner."

Emma leaned back against the seat, her eyes closed. "Couldn't we just catch a movie in Temptation? I'm afraid I worked too hard today and wouldn't be much company on the long drive to and from Dallas." She stared across the seat at Cooper, the sun glinting off her hair, casting a halo around her face.

Cooper swallowed hard. She was so beautiful and she didn't seem to know that simple fact. Such a change from the women who chased after him once they knew he was loaded. "I'm game for a movie. Wanna catch dinner first?"

"Are you hungry now, or could you wait until after the movie?"

"I can wait. I ate a late lunch."

"Good, I just want to relax."

Cooper pulled up to the only theater in Temptation and sat behind the wheel staring up at the posters. "Looks like we have two choices. An action flick or a romance. What's your poison?" He glanced sideways at Emma.

Emma opened her eyes and rolled her head toward him. "Action."

The thought of sitting in a darkened movie theater with Emma snuggled up against him made Cooper's pulse quicken. He leaped from the truck and rounded to her side.

Emma perched on the edge of the seat, her long tapered legs reaching for the running board.

"Allow me." Cooper clasped her around her narrow waist and swung her to the ground and into his arms where he held her for a long moment, inhaling the essence of Emma.

She rested her hands on his chest. "I thought we were going to a movie."

"Umm. Right." He took her hand and led her to the ticket window, where he bought two tickets to a spy thriller.

Once inside, they settled back as the movie started.

From the opening scene, Cooper knew the movie was a really bad idea and the feeling got worse with each passing minute.

A highly trained squad of soldiers moved through a mountain village searching for insurgents.

Beside Cooper, Emma tensed.

In the movie, a grenade landed in the middle of the shelled-out building the soldiers were searching and rolled to a stop in front of their leader.

"Run!" the leader shouted.

In the next moment, the man threw himself over the grenade.

Emma's hand reached out and grasped Cooper's arm, her fingers digging into Cooper's sleeve.

He took her hand and leaned close. "Let's go."

Emma let him lead her out of the theater. She hadn't uttered a word and when they exited the building into the balmy night air, she drew in a long steady breath and let it out.

"Are you okay?" Cooper asked.

She nodded. "Yes." As soon as the word left her lip, her head shook back and forth. "No."

"I'm sorry. Had I known, I wouldn't have taken you to that movie." Cooper turned her to face him.

Her head dipped. "It's okay."

"No, it's not." Cooper studied her pale face, then grabbed her hand. "Come on, let's walk."

If this truly was their last date, the last night together before their fake split, he'd completely blown it by taking her to see the carnage that only reminded Emma of how her fiancé had died. The damage done, he could only hope to cheer her up before taking her home and saying a final goodbye. "Where would you like to go?"

She walked several paces before responding. "Are you familiar with Temptation?"

"Not really." He turned to study her face in the glow of the streetlights.

She blinked then smiled, the effort stiff, but admirable. "Let me give you the fifty-cent tour."

They strolled along Main Street, Emma pointing out the stores and naming every owner, clerk and family member, painting a picture with her words of the quaint little town.

The more she talked, the steadier her voice became.

As they neared the end of the street and town, she stopped. "That's it. Now you know all there is to know about Temptation."

"You must love it here."

She shrugged. "I never wanted to live anywhere else."

Cooper tipped his head. "Wouldn't you have moved from post to post..." he caught his last words before they escaped, but it was too late.

"If Marcus had lived?" Emma nodded. "Yes, I would have moved from place to place, but my heart would have belonged to this little corner of Texas. We would have returned here after he retired."

"You still miss him." His words weren't a question, but more of a statement. He was beginning to realize just how much Emma had loved the soldier. "He was a very lucky man."

Emma snorted. "He's dead."

"Yeah, but he died knowing you loved him."

"Let's not talk about him." Emma spun away. "He's gone and never coming back."

Cooper rested his hands on her shoulders and turned her back to face him. "No, he's not, and I'm truly sorry for your loss."

Emma leaned her forehead against his chest, her fingers curling in his neatly starched shirt. "Thank you for understanding."

Cooper's hands slid down her arms and circled around her back, drawing her closer. "He was a brave man."

"Yes, he was." Emma's head tipped upward, allowing the overhead light to glint off her pupils, making them shine like stars. She leaned up on her toes and pressed her lips to Cooper's.

When she dropped back down, Cooper smiled. "What was that for?"

"My brothers are right."

"Yeah?"

"Cooper Johnson, you're a good man." She leaned back in his arms. "Most men would have pushed for more. You didn't."

"I don't force myself on women."

"My point exactly." She brushed his lips again and stepped free of his arms. "Are you going to feed me, or do I have to wait until I get home?"

Cooper let go of the breath he'd been holding and relaxed. "What's open in Temptation at this hour?"

"How are you with pizza?"

"I like it anyway it comes, except vegetarian."

"Good. I know a great little pizzeria on the other side of town." She captured his hand and set off, leading the way, her pretty yellow dress brushing against his fingers. "What's your favorite topping?"

Ace had told Cooper Emma's favorite topping was pepperoni. "I could go for a pepperoni." He hesitated and finished, "but I prefer the works."

Emma smiled up at him. "Marcus loved pepperoni and we always ordered it plain."

"We can do that, if you like."

"No." She shook her head. "I'd rather have all the toppings."

Cooper grinned. "I love the explosion of flavors in every bite."

"Me too." She laughed and hooked her arm through his, leaning into his body. "You know, you're all right for a desk-jockey cowboy. If I was even remotely interested in starting a relationship, I'd seriously consider you."

They walked the rest of the way across town, arm-in-arm. At the pizzeria, Cooper purchased a hand-tossed, pizza pie with everything, to go.

Emma tilted her head. "To go?"

"The stars are out, the air's not too hot or cold

and there's supposed to be a meteor shower tonight. I thought we'd head out past the city lights."

"I like that idea." She walked alongside him, her hands in her pockets.

With his own hands full of a pizza box, Cooper could do nothing more than match her pace. As they passed an alley between two buildings, a lonely mewling sound caught his attention. "Did you hear that?"

Emma stopped and looked up at Cooper, brow wrinkled. "What?"

Cooper stood still and listened. After several long moments of silence, he'd about credited the sound to the wind or his imagination. He shrugged and stepped forward when he heard it again. "That."

"Yes. I heard it that time." Emma spun to face the alley. "Sounded like it was coming from that direction."

"Mind holding this?" He held out the pizza box.

"Not at all."

Once he'd passed off possession of the box, he edged into the alley, his head tipped to the side.

"Hello?" he called out softly.

The mewling sounds grew louder and Cooper zeroed in on a box lying next to a trash bin.

"What is it?" Emma called out from the street.

"I don't know." He opened the box and peered inside.

Nestled in a dirty rag was a tiny calico kitten that

let out a pathetic wail and launched itself at Cooper's arm, spitting and hissing.

"Whoa there, little one." Cooper chuckled and plucked the kitten's claws out of his sleeve and stood.

Emma, still carrying the pizza box, appeared at his side. "What is it—oh, a kitten."

"Appears to have been dumped." Cooper nudged the box into the light. Written in bold, but childish, letters were the words, *Please give me a home.*

Cooper had only to stroke the kitten's soft fur once to know he couldn't leave it there. Ace had mentioned Emma liked dogs, not cats, and he didn't want to put her on the spot with the tiny creature. "Guess I've just inherited a kitten."

"Still want to go watch the stars?" Emma asked.

He tucked the frightened kitten into the crook of one arm and petted him until he closed his eyes and slept. "I'm game as long as Lucky is."

Emma's heart swelled as she stared at the tall, dark and handsome man cuddling the defenseless kitten. "I thought most men hated cats."

"I'm not most men." He tickled the kitten beneath the chin. "And this little guy doesn't deserve to be tossed in the trash." He reached for the pizza box. "Want me to get that?"

"I can carry this." Emma retained her hold on the box and fell in step beside Cooper. When they reached the truck, still parked at the theater on Main, Emma turned to face him. "So, where to?"

"Out of town was as far as I got with the idea."

Emma grinned. "I know a place."

"The Rockin' J?"

"No. I have somewhere else in mind." She held out her hand. "Trust me to drive your truck?"

CHAPTER 9

EMMA WAITED, wondering if Cooper would balk at a woman driving his vehicle. Marcus had always insisted on driving, never once letting Emma behind the wheel of his truck.

"Sure." Cooper fished in his pocket for the keys and handed them over, no mention of being careful or a single frown of consternation accompanied his gesture.

Her heart lightening, Emma hit the button to unlock the doors, laid the pizza box on the back seat and climbed into the driver's side, adjusting the seat so she could reach the brake and gas pedal.

Cooper eased into the passenger seat, the kitten snuggled close to his white shirt, content to be held and rubbed.

Emma headed west out of town toward the Rockin' J, passing the arched gate without slowing.

After crossing the bridge over Willow Creek, she turned in at the top of the next rise and pulled to a stop at an old gate with a rusty hinges. A *For Sale* sign clung to the fence beside the gate, with a *No Trespassing* sign hanging sideways by a single wire beneath it.

"I take it you know the owner?" Cooper asked as he climbed down, still holding the kitten.

"I do. He doesn't mind me visiting as long as I close the gates behind me."

"Glad to hear that. Hate to think of someone shooting me and Lucky for trespassing." With one hand, Cooper unhooked the chain looped over the fence post and swung the gate wide, closing it after Emma drove his truck through.

Emma had rolled down the windows and sat patiently while Cooper climbed back into the truck. Already, she felt as if she'd just come home. She loved this little piece of Texas heaven and couldn't wait to call it her own. She drove to the highest rise where a cottage perched, the windows dark, not a single vehicle parked nearby.

"Abandoned?" Cooper asked.

"For now." Emma smiled at the house with the crooked porch. "Just needs the right owner to bring it back to life."

"Have one in mind?"

"Maybe," she whispered softly. Pulling up in front

of the house, she shifted into park and climbed down. "If Old Man Rausch doesn't sell it too soon."

"I keep a sleeping bag tucked behind the back seat for emergencies. We could use it as our picnic blanket." Cooper climbed down from the passenger side and opened the crew cab and rummaged in a gym bag, dragging out a clean white T-shirt.

"What's that for?" Emma grabbed the pizza box and tipped the backseat forward.

"Lucky." Cooper wadded up the shirt on the floorboard and laid the kitten inside. "I think he'll sleep for a while. If not, we'll hear him through the open windows."

Emma smiled at how carefully Cooper handled the kitten. "Marcus didn't like cats."

"And you?"

"Never had one, other than the strays in the barn that kept down the mouse population." She grinned. "And for the record—I think all calicos are female."

Cooper's brows lifted and he stared across the seat at Emma. "Lucky's a girl?"

"That would be my guess."

"Lucky again, aren't you?" Cooper patted the cat. "The name isn't gender specific."

While Cooper retrieved the sleeping bag, Emma carried the pizza box to the middle of the front yard, a prime location for viewing the stars. Even the house didn't block much of the sky.

Cooper spread the sleeping bag on the grass and took the pizza box from Emma while she settled.

Up until that point, Emma had been completely relaxed and comfortable with Cooper. Once she stretched out on the flannel lining of the bag, her heart flipped several times. She could imagine Cooper lying naked in the bag, beside a campfire, staring up at the clear, starlit night. Even more alarming, she could picture herself lying beside him…equally disrobed.

The pizza box was the only barrier that could come between them in this scenario, and Cooper laid it at the foot of the shared blanket.

"If you're hungry, go ahead and help yourself." He laid back and stared up at the night sky. "Like I said, I had a late lunch."

"I can wait." Emma eased onto her side, staring more at the man than the sky, wondering whether he'd make a move to pull her into his arms. Or worse, that he wouldn't. The familiar guilt only slightly nudged her this time, and that fact scared her more than the thought of Cooper kissing her.

Her lips tingled, the night air warming around her.

Cooper pointed at the sky. "Look. Venus, Jupiter and Mars are all in alignment."

"Where?" Emma lay down on her back and stared up at the sky.

The cowboy scooted closer and pointed at the stars. "The ones shining brighter than the others."

His nearness made Emma's breath lodge in her chest. "I'm not seeing them."

"Here, lean on my arm." He slipped his arm beneath her head and pointed again.

By that time, Emma couldn't think past the solid muscle beneath her neck or the fresh scent of his soap and the long, hard length of his body stretched out beside hers.

"See it?" he whispered, his breath skimming across her temple.

"Oh, yes," she said, her gaze on him, not the sky. They could have been lying in a barn for all the attention she could afford the stars. Her pulse hammered against her eardrums, and she tilted her head to the side, her cheek resting on his shoulder.

God, being in a man's arms felt good.

No. She was wrong.

Being in *Cooper's* arms felt great.

"I'm always amazed..." Cooper turned to face her, his lips only inches from hers, his words fading away.

"Amazed?" Emma asked, shocked at how breathy the word came out of her mouth.

"At how beautiful..." His tongue brushed across his lips and he inhaled, then curled his arm, bringing her closer. "How beautiful you are." His lips brushed over hers in a feather-soft kiss.

Emma laughed, breathily. "I thought we were talking about the stars."

"To hell with the stars." Cooper came up on his elbow and leaned over her body. "Do you realize what you're doing to me?"

"No." As if of its own accord, her hand rose to caress Cooper's cheek, the hint of rough stubble sending shivers of awareness across her skin. "Tell me."

"I can't be a gentleman forever." He brushed a tendril of hair from her forehead. "Not with you."

She dragged in a deep breath and let it go, along with her hesitation to make love to this man. "Then what are you waiting for?"

Cooper's eyes flared, then his mouth crashed down over hers, his tongue sweeping past her teeth to claim her own.

She matched him stroke for stroke, as she flicked open the buttons of his shirt, baring his chest to her marauding hands.

Cooper slid his fingers across her cheek, down the curve of her neck and across a breast, capturing it in his palm.

Emma arched her back, pressing deeper into his grip. She wanted to be closer, to feel his skin against hers.

His hand slipped lower to the hem of her dress and he paused, his lips leaving hers. "Tell me to stop, and I will."

"No. Please, don't stop." She couldn't give herself time to think, afraid she'd come up with a dozen good reasons not to make love to Cooper. Emma guided his fingers to the hem and helped him pull it up her body and over her head. The warm, balmy air caressed her skin, making her deliciously aware of her near nakedness and wanting to take the next step.

She attacked the remaining buttons on Cooper's shirt and slid it over his broad shoulders, her fingers gliding across his smooth, tight muscles.

Fire raged in her blood, urging her to move faster, reaching for the buckle on his belt.

Cooper got there first and ripped open the belt, then the hook on his trousers.

Emma's fingers closed around the zipper and slid it downward, ever so slowly, her knuckles grazing the hard ridge beneath. His member sprang free into her hand—hard, straight and velvety smooth.

All the long, lonely nights lying alone merged with the pent-up desire building inside her since meeting this man and burst to the surface. Emma pushed Cooper to his back and yanked off his boots and trousers. Then she straddled his hips and reached for the hooks on the back of her bra.

He grabbed her arms and held her steady. "Hey, slow down."

"I can't." Staring into his gaze, she flicked the hooks, her breasts spilling free from the lace.

His gaze didn't slip from hers. "I want you to be sure about this."

"I'm sure." With deliberate moves, Emma shrugged out of his hold and let her bra straps slide down her arms to the blanket.

Then she grasped his hands and guided them to her naked breasts. "Am I unattractive naked?" She froze, waiting for him to take the lead, her heart pounding against her ribs, fear clutching at gut. Now that he had her so close, would he still want her? Or would he be repulsed by her forwardness and her body?

Cooper shook his head, a smile curling his lips.

For a moment, Emma's heart stopped.

Then he bucked beneath her and flipped her onto her back. "Emma Jacobs, I've wanted you since the moment we met. I want you so much I ache with it."

Emma released the breath she'd been holding, swallowed hard on a sob and twined her hands around his neck. "Then kiss me."

He lowered his mouth to claim hers in a kiss so tender it melted Emma's insides.

His hand swept away her panties, the warm, calloused fingers, scraping her skin in a sensuous glide. Then he parted her legs with his knee and slipped between them.

The kiss lasted until Emma thought she might never need to breathe again. Then Cooper's lips skimmed across her chin and down the length of her throat, to the turgid peak of her right nipple. He nibbled and laved, then sucked the tip between his lips.

Emma arched off the blanket, pushing her breast deeper into his warm, wet mouth. Every part of her body tingled with electric shocks, the tension building, heating up at her core.

Cooper abandoned her breasts and moved lower, pressing kisses to each of her ribs, his tongue dipping into her belly button. His steady path downward ignited an inferno inside her.

When Cooper reached the thatch of curls covering Emma's sex, she drew up a knee and braced herself for what might come next.

With broad, coarse fingers, he parted her folds and stroked the little swollen bundle of nerves at her center.

Emma gasped, her bottom rising off the ground, her fingers threading through Cooper's dark hair.

The world stood still as Cooper touched his tongue to her most sensitive spot.

"Oh, dear God," she cried out, her fingers clenching against his scalp.

He flicked her again, sending a shower of shocks shooting throughout her body. Tingling began in her toes and fingers, speeding through her arms into her body and soul.

She rose to meet his next assault, unprepared for the exquisite torture of his mouth claiming her, sucking her in. Every muscle solidified. Emma forgot how to breathe, forgot where she was and gave herself up to the explosion of sensations raging through her.

Before she could regroup or rethink, Cooper released her and fumbled in the pocket of her dress, removing the dark foil package.

She took the packet from his fingers, tore it with her teeth and slipped the rubber down over his engorged cock. Then she spread her knees wide, grabbed his length and guided him into her channel.

He slid into her warm wetness, filling the emptiness she'd lived with for so long.

When he'd buried himself to the hilt, he stopped, holding steady, giving her time to adjust to his length and girth. Then he was moving in and out, picking up speed with each stroke.

Emma rose to meet his every thrust. She clutched his buttocks, making him pump harder, faster until he was pounding in and out of her body.

On one final thrust, he stopped, his body rigid, his eyes closed tight, his face tensed.

Inside, his cock throbbed against her channel.

Emma wrapped her legs around his waist and held him there, savoring their intimacy, the feel of his length inside, the sensation of his skin tight against hers.

When he finally relaxed, Cooper dropped to the blanket beside her, turning her on her side without breaking their connection. Then he kissed her again, his lips soft against hers. "You're amazing."

She slid her leg up over his thigh. "Not so bad yourself."

The longer they lay there, the more the cool night air chilled Emma's body and with it, the memories crowded in, bringing the guilt.

Cooper slipped free of her and she let her leg fall to her side.

Heat filled her cheeks as the reality of what she'd done set in. She sat up and reached for her clothes. "We'd better go."

Cooper sat up behind her, brushed her hair back from her neck and pressed a kiss to the column of her throat. "You know this changes everything, don't you?"

Shaking her head, Emma sucked in a long breath, squeezing her eyes closed. "Why does it have to change anything?"

His hand stilled on her shoulder. "I don't understand."

"Nothing to understand." Clutching her clothes in her hands, she stood.

Cooper grabbed his trousers and stood, dragging them up over his legs. "You're wrong."

"I told you from the beginning, I didn't want a relationship. This was our last date."

He gripped her shoulders and leaned down to her

eye level. "Look at me and tell me what just happened meant nothing."

Her chest aching, and a sob rising up her throat, Emma looked away. "Why does what we did have to mean something?"

"Because it did." He shook her gently. "Emma, look at me."

She did, her vision clouded by the tears welling in her eyes. She'd loved Marcus, but Cooper was so alive and vibrant and here. If she chose him over Marcus, she'd betray her love. "I loved Marcus. Don't make me choose between the two of you."

"I'm not asking you to choose. Marcus is dead. I'm not." He breathed a steadying breath and continued, "I want you, and I'm well on my way to falling in love. But I can't compete with a memory. Do you or don't you have room in your heart for me?"

Emma hesitated, her world shattering into a million pieces.

Cooper waited for several seconds, then his hands fell from her shoulders. "Forget I said anything. I'll stick to the bargain. Tomorrow, you can tell your brothers that I was a jerk. I don't care. Just end it." He scooped up his shirt and boots and marched to the truck, leaving Emma standing on the sleeping bag, tears arrested, refusing to fall.

A heavy weight lodged deep in her chest. What had she done?

CHAPTER 10

As soon as Cooper pulled up at her front door, Emma hopped out of the truck. At well past midnight, the lights were out in the living room and not one of her brothers waited on the porch to make sure she got home safely.

Before she could escape, Cooper rounded the truck and grabbed her hand. "Emma, wait."

"Don't." She tugged her hand, but couldn't break his grasp.

"I walked into this experiment skeptical, but I'm glad I did." He lifted her hand to his lips and pressed a kiss into her palm. "No matter what happens, I'll never regret having met you." Then he let go, climbed into his truck and drove away.

Emma slipped into the house, padding barefoot down the hallway to her room. As she was closing the door, Nelson slipped in.

Then the flood gates opened, tears fell and silent sobs shook her body. She crawled into her bed, still wearing the yellow dress and cried.

Nelson stood beside the bed, nudging her hand and whining softly.

A soft knock on the door didn't faze her. Emma couldn't stop the flow of sadness.

"Emma?" Ace's voice sounded through wooden panels.

Too lost in her own misery to care, she didn't respond.

The door opened and Ace entered, followed by Brand, Colton and Dillon.

"What happened?" Ace sat on the edge of the mattress.

"Nothing," Emma sobbed.

"Want me to beat him up?" Brand asked.

"I'll get my shotgun," Colton said. "Just say the word."

"No." She rolled her face into the pillow. "Just leave me alone."

None of them moved.

"Go!" she wailed and threw a pillow in their direction.

Footsteps padded away, and the door closed.

And she was alone again. Emma rolled onto her back and stared at the ceiling, then turned to face the photo on the nightstand, her fingers reaching for the edge of the frame. "Marcus, what should I do?"

Nelson nudged her extended hand and the photo tipped over, face-down.

Emma froze. "Marcus?" A breeze lifted the curtains at the window and brushed across her skin like a kiss. "I really did love you," she whispered and curled around the empty pillow in the bed beside her. The photograph remained face-down, as Emma drifted off into a deep, dreamless sleep.

COOPER LAY in his bed wide awake all night long. Lucky lay against his side, curled into a tight, colorful fur ball.

As much as he wanted to be with Emma, Cooper could tell the choice between him and her dead fiancé was pulling her apart. By morning, he'd made up his mind.

He tucked the kitten into his shirt pocket, stopped by the pet store in Temptation and bought a small animal pet carrier, a bag of kitty chow, another bag of litter and a tray and headed to the Rockin' J Ranch. The trip was the longest and the shortest of his life.

As he pulled up in the yard, Ace stepped out on the porch, followed by Brand. Colton and Dillon rounded the side of the house and met their brothers at the bottom of the stairs. All four men crossed their arms and glared at Cooper.

Cooper eased down from his truck and stepped into the fray. "Is Emma home?"

"What did you do to her?" Dillon leaned forward, his hands clenching into fists.

"Why do you ask?" Cooper frowned. "What did she say?'

"She didn't say anything but she cried all night long." Brand joined Dillon, flexing his broad shoulders, his fists clenched, ready to throw a punch.

Cooper didn't care. A punch in the face couldn't hurt any more than what he was about to do. "Relax. I came to break it off with Emma. Let me talk to her, and I'll leave."

"Is that why she cried all night, because you broke her heart?" Colton pushed up his sleeves. "I'm gonna kick your ass all the way back to Dallas."

Cooper sighed. "No, I didn't break off our relationship."

"Why should we believe you?" Brand demanded.

"Believe what you want. Truth is, I made the mistake of telling her I was falling in love with her."

"Right." Dillon stepped closer, raising his fists. "And that's why she cried her eyes out last night."

Colton joined Dillon and Brand. "You'll have to do better than that if you don't want an ass whooping."

Lucky chose that moment to poke his head out of Cooper's pocket.

Cooper smiled down at the spunky little cat. "You wouldn't hit a man carrying a kitten, would you?"

"I'll deck anyone who makes my sister cry," Dillon said.

Ace pushed through his brothers. "Leave him alone."

"Are you believing his story?" Dillon turned on his brother.

With a twisted smile, Ace nodded. "Yeah. I do."

Cooper brushed a hand across his forehead, really relieved he had at least one of the Jacobs on his side. "Thanks. These guys had me sweating." He stared past Ace toward the house, his gut tightening. "Is she here?"

"She's out riding. Left before any of us got out of bed."

Disappointment dragged Cooper's shoulders down. He had hoped to see her one last time, but maybe their situation was better this way. If he saw her, he'd only want to hold her until she pried his fingers loose. "Do you mind if I leave her a note?" He glanced down at the kitten as she climbed his shirt. "And the kitten."

Still glaring, Dillon shot back, "We're not big cat people around here."

"We found it last night. Emma seemed taken with Lucky." Cooper glanced into Ace's eyes. "Sounds like she needs the company."

"She has Nelson," Dillon reminded.

"Yeah, but a girl could use more than one friend." Ace took the kitten from Cooper. "Lucky, huh?"

"If we hadn't walked down Main Street in Temptation, we wouldn't have found her, trapped in a box. She might have died."

Lucky swatted at Ace, claws unsheathed.

"Whoa, Tiger." He held the kitten out for Cooper. "Maybe you should take her. Apparently, she doesn't care for me."

"She grows on you." Cooper retrieved the kitten and glanced toward the side of the house, hoping Emma would turn up before he left.

"You sure you want to break it off with Emma?"

"It's what she wants."

"And you?"

Cooper bit back the truth and glanced down at the kitten, avoiding Ace's gaze. "It's what she wants."

Ace snorted. "Based on the tears last night and her riding out this morning, I'd say Emma doesn't know what Emma wants."

"Trust me, if there was a way to bring her around, I'd gladly listen." Cooper glanced up hopefully. "Maybe if you talked to her…"

Ace's lips pressed together and he shook his head. "If there's one thing I know about my sister, she has to come around on her own. If you want to leave her a note, you can. I'm still skeptical about the kitten."

Cooper nodded, hope fading. He retrieved the cat

supplies from his truck and the note he'd crafted before he'd left his house.

Ace led him through the front door and down the hallway, pushing open a door. "You can leave the note in her room. The cat too, since you brought along a kennel."

"Thanks." Cooper paused on the threshold. Stepping inside made him feel like he was trespassing on Emma's personal space.

"Go on. I'm sure she'd rather read the note in private. I'll leave you alone."

"Thanks." Cooper swallowed hard on the lump lodged in his throat. "I'll make it quick."

"Take your time." Ace half-closed the door and retreated back the way he'd come.

Cooper stared around at the bedroom with the wide windows overlooking the backyard, stretching past the fences to a pasture still tall with Bermuda hay, ready for baling. Too bad, he wouldn't be around to help with the chore. He'd enjoyed working beside the Jacobs two days ago.

A hollowness grew in Cooper's belly. Knowing this would be the last time he'd be around her brothers and this would be his last contact with Emma left him empty and sad.

No matter how many times he reminded himself that he'd known her only a very short time, he couldn't believe he'd never see her again. In the few days he'd known Emma, she'd made a lasting impression, one that would remain a very long time and shape how he viewed other women. She'd set the bar so high, no other woman could reach it.

As he glanced around the room, he could see evidence of Emma in everything. The pictures on the wall, the quilt on the bed, the scent lingering in the air.

He set the pet carrier on the bed, the litter box, the bags of litter and cat food on the floor and pulled the note out of his back pocket.

Lucky clung to his shirt, as if sensing she was about to be left behind yet again.

"Don't worry. Emma will take good care of you. She has more love in her heart than even she knows." He plucked the cat's claws out of the fabric, stroked its little head and set the calico kitten inside the carrier, shutting the door before she could escape.

"Take care of her." He laid the envelope containing his note on the bed and backed away. That's when he noticed the photo frame lying face-down on the nightstand.

Out of instinct, he set the frame upright, unprepared for the punch in the gut.

Emma's face glowed with happiness as she smiled at a man with a military haircut.

Marcus.

Cooper backed out of the room, his heart squeezing hard, his lungs refusing to allow air in and out.

"Anything else you want us to tell Emma?" Ace intercepted Cooper as he made for the door.

"No," was all he could push past the muscles constricting his throat.

Ace stuck out his hand. "We had high hopes things would turn out better. Sorry."

Cooper shook the man's hand and left without another word.

As he drove away, he glanced in the rearview mirror with the final hope of seeing Emma ride in on her horse.

Her brothers had streamed out onto the porch, their gazes following his truck.

No Emma.

With nothing left to do, Cooper focused ahead and tried to forget about the woman who'd so easily captured his heart.

As Emma rode into the barnyard, Dillon appeared from around the side of the house, his hands jammed into his front pockets, his face downcast. "You had a visitor."

Her heart leaped and she swung down from the saddle. "Who?" Even before her brother answered, she knew.

Cooper.

She handed her reins to Dillon and pushed past him toward the house.

"He's gone."

Dillon's voice halted Emma. Her racing heart screeched to a fluttering stop as she turned to face her youngest brother. "Why did he come?"

"To break up with you." Dillon's eyes narrowed. "A cryin' shame if you ask me. I kinda liked the man."

So, there it was. Cooper had done what she'd asked. Emma should have felt relieved. She'd gotten exactly what she'd wanted. Maybe now, her brothers would leave her alone about dating. Emma should have felt satisfied, but all she could muster was a cold, empty feeling in the center of her chest.

"He left a note in your room."

Dillon's voice lanced through the fog edging in around her, and Emma's head jerked up. "What?"

"In your room, Cooper left a note."

She spun on her boot heels and ran across the yard and in through the backdoor. Ace stepped out of her way as she raced down the hallway to her room.

A soft mewling sound hit her as she entered, and Emma's knees almost buckled, a sob rising up her throat.

Lucky peered at her through the metal mesh of the pet carrier.

Emma freed the kitten and cuddled her against her chin, tears trickling down to land on the animal's soft fur.

"Aren't you going to read the note?" Ace said from the doorway.

Emma's gaze shifted to the envelope propped against her pillow. She snatched it up with her free hand and opened it awkwardly, balancing the kitten. A single page fluttered out and landed on the night-stand next to the photo of her and Marcus.

Marcus was a lucky man and would have been proud of your undying love. I concede this battle to him, unable to compete for your love against such a heartfelt memory.

PS. Figured you could use a little Luck. Take care of her, and remember that everyone needs a little love. Even you.

Emma clutched the note and the kitten to her chest.

Cooper was gone. She'd pushed away the one man able to rekindle her desire and hope for the future. Emma felt as if she'd been asleep for a long time and finally woken up. Cooper had been respon-sible for that. How could she let him walk away?

The tears dried and her fingers tightened around the paper. Her pulse quickened and she spun to face Ace. "How long ago did he leave?"

"He left just before you rode into the barnyard," Ace said. "Driving pretty slowly, too. I think he was hoping to see you."

Emma shoved the kitten into Ace's arms. "Hold Lucky." She shoved past him and ran down the hall.

"Do I have a choice?" Ace called out behind her.

Emma didn't answer. She didn't have a choice. She had to catch Cooper and tell him how she felt.

That he'd come to mean more than a fake date. That he'd brought her back from a living death. That she didn't want to go another day without him in her life. If she had to, she'd beg him to give her another chance. If she could catch him before he got away. Because for the first time since she'd started down the online dating path, she realized she didn't have his phone number or address.

The road leading into the ranch house forced travelers to move slowly. If she shot over the ridge and down the hill, she might catch him on the farm road that connected to the main highway. She'd have to go cross-country.

Dillon was just heading into the barn with Emma's palomino in tow.

"Wait!" Emma cried out.

Daisy tossed her head and backed away from the barn door.

Dillon swung around. "What's wrong?"

"I need that horse." She didn't slow as she raced toward the barn. Snatching the reins from her bewildered brother, Emma leaped into the saddle, turned the horse and dug her heels into the animal's flanks. Woman and beast blew through the open gate and into the pasture.

Daisy stretched her neck, her hooves bunching and spreading beneath her.

The wind in Emma's face blew away the last of

her doubts. She hoped and prayed Cooper hadn't completely given up.

As the far fence line came into view, Emma glanced to the east. A truck barreled along the farm road toward the T-intersection of the main highway leading back to Temptation and ultimately Dallas.

Emma urged Daisy faster, bending over her neck, one with the horse.

The animal responded, ears laid back, hooves flying low over the mowed field.

When they came within twenty yards of the fence, Emma sat back in the saddle and pulled on the reins.

Daisy ground to a halt, inches from the barbed wire.

Emma threw herself from the saddle, climbed over the fence and ran the one hundred yards to the intersection stretching before her like an eternity. Heart racing, pulse pounding, her lungs burning, she realized she wasn't going to make it.

Cooper would turn to the left before she reached him. He'd drive off and Emma would never see him again.

She picked up her knees and elbows and ran faster.

The truck slowed to a stop at the convergence of the two highways and a strange thing happened.

The vehicle didn't budge.

Cooper didn't turn. For several long moments,

the truck remained in place, granting Emma more time to catch up.

Then the truck lurched forward, swinging left. The brake lights glowed bright red and the white reverse lights engaged.

Cooper was backing up and turning around!

Emma stumbled and almost cried in her relief. She angled toward the farm road, dipped down in the roadside ditch and up onto the pavement, running right in front of the pickup.

Tires squealed, and the truck skidded to a stop, but not soon enough.

The hood of the truck bumped her just enough to send her crashing to the ground. Pain shot through her hip where she landed, but Emma didn't care as she dragged air into her lungs.

"Emma!" The driver's door flung open and Cooper was beside her. "Holy hell, woman. Are you all right?"

She dragged in another breath and nodded. "I am now."

"You scared the crap out of me. What are you trying to do, get yourself killed?"

"Had…to…" she sucked in a breath and finished, "stop you."

"And that was worth throwing yourself in front of a moving vehicle?" He gathered her into his arms. "You're insane."

She pressed her face into his shirt and laughed. "I am. Insane to think I can start over."

"What are you talking about?" He leaned back enough to stare into her eyes.

"Insane to think you'd give me another chance." She cupped his face and smiled upward. "Now that we've established I'm insane, could you possibly buy into that insanity plea and give me another chance?"

For a long moment, he stared into her eyes. "I was coming back to beg you for that chance."

"Thank God." Emma cupped her palms around his face and leaned up to kiss him.

After a long, deep kiss, Cooper broke it off. "What about Marcus?"

"He'll always be a part of me." She inhaled and let it out. "A part of my past. But I have to keep on living. I have a future, one that I hope includes you."

"Baby, that's what I wanted to hear." He rose, lifted her into his arms and carried her to his truck. "Hopefully, now we don't have to break up our little family."

Emma laughed. "Lucky?"

"I'm feeling it, are you?"

She wrapped her arms around his neck and kissed him soundly. "How are you with a woman who wants to own her own spread?"

"I'd buy it for you, if I knew it would make you happy."

"I could never accept such an expensive gift." She shook her head. "I want to pay for it myself."

He kissed the tip of her nose. "Your determination and independence is one of the things I love most about you."

"Your patience and understanding is what I love about you." Emma grinned. "And you do have a very nice ass."

He kissed her again, stealing her breath away with his tenderness.

Then they were on their way back to the Rockin' J Ranch and a house full of stunned brothers. A warm breeze wafted through the open window, brushing across Emma's face.

For a moment, she closed her eyes and sent a silent prayer to the heavens, "Thank you, Marcus."

EPILOGUE

Cooper stood at the head of the conference room table, having called an emergency meeting of Billionaires Anonymous.

"Well?" Tag drummed his fingers on the table. "What's the emergency?"

"Wait for our guest." Cooper waved a hand toward the door.

Leslie Lamb entered, her eyes wide, appearing as confused by the short notice as the others. "What's going on?"

"I wanted my friends to be witness as I write out a check."

Leslie's brow furrowed, then climbed up her forehead, her eyes widening. "You and Emma?"

Cooper nodded and called out. "You can come in."

Emma entered through another doorway, a grin

splitting her face. She gave a shy wave to the men gathered around. "Hi."

As one, Sean, Tag, Maxwell and Gage whistled.

"You lucky bastard," Gage was the first to reach him and pound him on the back. "Nice to meet you, Emma. Coop's had only good things to say about you."

Emma took all the well-wishes and ribbing with a smile while Cooper almost busted buttons on his shirt, he was so proud.

Leslie was last to hug Emma. "I'm happy for you, sweetie."

Emma hugged her back, swiping at a tear in her eye. "Thanks for kicking my butt into taking a chance."

"Don't thank me, thank that big cowboy of yours." Leslie stood back, smiling broadly. "If he hadn't been the right match, things might not have worked out so well."

"Which brings me back to this." Cooper waved his checkbook. "I'm here to write a check for every cent in my back account."

"Holy cow, Coop." Tag shook his head. "Have you lost your mind?"

"Better, I've lost my heart." With a happy groan, he pulled Emma into his arms. "How can you put a price on that?"

Leslie raised her hands. "I won't take it. Look, I'll

send you a bill for a reasonable amount. No offense, Emma."

Emma chuckled. "None taken."

"The main thing I need from you, Mr. Johnson" — Leslie crossed her arms and cocked an eyebrow— "is a referral."

"You got it," Cooper said, as he smiled down at Emma.

"And you have mine, as well." Emma stared up into Cooper's eyes, heating the air between them. "I'll have to get my brothers signed up right away."

"Great!" Leslie turned to the other men gathered around and clapped her hands. "So... who's next?"

THE END

Enjoy other books by Elle James

Billionaire Online Dating Service
The Billionaire Husband Test (#1)
The Billionaire Cinderella Test (#2)
The Billionaire Bride Test (#3) TBD
The Billionaire Matchmaker Test (#4) TBD
Texas Billionaire Club
Tarzan & Janine (#1)
Something To Talk About (#2)
Who's Your Daddy (#3)
Love & War (#4)

Visit ellejames.com for more titles and release dates
For hot cowboys, visit her alter ego Myla Jackson at
mylajackson.com
and join Elle James and Myla Jackson's Newsletter at
http://ellejames.com/ElleContact.htm

THE BILLIONAIRE CINDERELLA TEST

BILLIONAIRE ONLINE DATING SERVICE
BOOK #2

New York Times & *USA Today*
Bestselling Author

ELLE JAMES

BILLIONAIRE

Cinderella
Test
BILLIONAIRE ONLINE DATING SERVICE

ELLE JAMES
NEW YORK TIMES BESTSELLING AUTHOR

CHAPTER 1

"WE GOT A PROBLEM, BOSS."

Gage Tate clenched his teeth and held his temper. "What now?"

"The replacement boom we contracted didn't show up this morning."

Not good. Of all days for work on the Platinum Towers to grind to a halt, now was not a good one. "Did you call and find out why?"

Marcus Shipley nodded. "Yup. He said he didn't have one available until a week from today."

"And when was he going to tell us?"

Marcus's lips twisted around the toothpick that had replaced cigarettes in his mouth. "A week from today."

"We can't come to a complete halt for an entire week. The delay on materials acquisition already set us two weeks behind schedule. Every day we go past our completion date costs us money."

"I have a call into another boom company; they think they can get one to us in two days. My contact said he'd let us know by the end of the day."

"Great. I have a meeting with Mr. Langley in exactly," he glanced at his watch, "ten minutes. Here. To show him what we're capable of. On a work site where no work is being done." Gage raked a hand through his hair.

"William Langley? The man who owns half of downtown Dallas?"

"Yes. That Langley. I want that property on the corner of Elm and Griffin Streets."

"I thought he didn't want to sell it to you on account of you hadn't paid your dues."

"I have to convince him I wasn't handed my money. I earned every last damn cent, unlike so many of his cronies." He glanced at the parking area, wishing he had time to call in a crew to at least look like they were busy making progress on the multi-million-dollar project slipping further and further behind.

Marcus's eyes widened. "Ain't that the lady you hired to improve your image?"

Gage followed his nod toward the woman in a pencil skirt marching toward him with purpose in her stride, even if she couldn't quite lengthen her stride in that ridiculous skirt.

Marcus tipped his head down, hiding his grin from the woman advancing on them. "How's that going for you?'

"What?" Gaged stalled, hating that he'd had to hire an image consultant in order to secure the desired property. "She thinks I'm too unapproachable. That I need to soften up and or get laid."

Marcus grinned. "That's my kind of consultant. Think she'd go for someone like me?"

"No." Gage braced himself for Haddie Madison, the fifty-year-old image consultant he'd hired out of desperation. Pasting on his most congenial face, he greeted her with a forced smile. "What brings you out to the job site, Ms. Madison?"

Her brows twisted. "Wow. That's the best you can do? I can see straight through that pathetic attempt at pleasantries. And, please, call me Haddie."

Gage abandoned the fake smile. "Haddie. What are you doing here?"

"You said you had a meeting with Mr. Langley today, in ten minutes, if I'm not mistaken."

"Eight."

She nodded. "I'm here for moral support and to observe your interaction with the man."

Marcus coughed to hide his snort of laughter.

Gage glared at him. "Get your crew busy on something, even if it's only cleaning up the work site."

Marcus let loose his grin and clapped a hand to Gage's back, nearly knocking him over. "And that's why you're paid the big bucks, my friend." The site foreman strolled away whistling. Not a care in the world, other than finding a boom to replace the one that had crapped out on them on the tenth floor of a ninety-story project.

"Ah, that must be Mr. Langley now." Haddie turned toward the limousine easing into the job site.

"If you're going to be here, you need to wear a hard hat." Gage reached into his work truck where he kept spares and handed her a scuffed, yellow hard hat.

Haddie sighed. "And I just had my hair done." Despite the damage to her hair, she settled the hat on her head and waited for the passenger of the limousine to alight.

Gage sucked in a deep breath. Nothing had gone right that morning. The boom hadn't arrived, Haddie had descended on him without warning and Langley had showed up on time. What more could go wrong?

The chauffeur parked, got out and opened the back door of the limousine and a bright turquoise blue stiletto emerged, followed by a long slender leg.

Gage groaned as Priscilla Langley unfolded her body from the back of the limo, flinging her long black hair back over her shoulder. Her father followed.

And that was what more could go wrong.

He'd invited Langley to the job site hoping to prove to the man he knew what he was doing and was capable of converting the man's eyesore of a building in downtown Dallas into a modern, designer structure that would bring more jobs and revenue to the city center. If only he'd leave his pain-in-the-ass daughter out of the equation.

Priscilla wobbled across the uneven gravel in her spike heels. "Gage, darling, I hope you don't mind, but Daddy insisted I come along." She held out her hand, her wrist limp like a queen expecting her subject to kiss her hand.

William Langley shook his head. "That's not how I remember it."

Gage gripped her hand and gave it a quick, firm shake. "Ms. Langley," he said, his lips stiff. He didn't need the drama of Langley's daughter distracting William from the reason he'd been invited there. When he released his hold on Priscilla's hand, she didn't let go of his.

Forced to peel her fingers off his, Gage finally shook loose and held out his hand to William Langley. "Mr. Langley, thank, you for coming out to the job site."

Haddie cleared her throat, a slight frown pinching her brow for a second before she extended her hand. "Hello, Mr. Langley, Haddie Madison. I'm Mr. Tate's consultant."

William smiled and shook her hand. "What kind of consultant might that be?"

Gage held his breath, waiting for Haddie to spill

the beans about his attempt to woo the great William Langley.

"Design consultant.," she said, her brows rising as she stared across at Gage. "I want this project to be the best it can be."

"This place is amazing." Priscilla walked toward the construction site. "Do you go up on those steel beams?"

Gage grabbed two hard hats from the back seat of his truck, handing one to William and hurrying after Priscilla with the other. "Ms. Langley, you have to wear a hard hat on the site."

She waved her manicured nails at him. "I don't need that. I never wear them on my father's work sites, do I, Daddy?" She smiled and blew a kiss at her father.

William Langley sighed. "I can't get her to do anything she doesn't want to do."

Gage held out the hat to the spoiled socialite. "Wear the hat or you'll have to stay in the limousine while we tour the site. I lose my liability insurance if anyone on the job site isn't wearing a hard hat."

Priscilla's pretty brow dented and her red painted lips pursed. "Daddy?"

Her father shrugged. "You can wait in the car if you don't want to mess up your hair."

"But I wanted to see what Gage is working on." She leaned into Gage and ran her fingers up the front of his shirt. "And to see if he has a date to his charity ball." She winked up at him, curling her fingers around his neck. "Do you?"

Anger burned a path from Gage's gut all the way up into his cheeks and threatened to explode out of the top of his head.

Haddie touched his arm and whispered, "Remember our project?"

The older woman's reminder clamped a lid on Gage's temper and he drew in a deep breath, untangled Priscilla's hands from around his neck and he said, "I'm sorry, I have a date to the charity ball. And since you don't want to wear your hat, I'm asking that you stay in the car while your father and I discuss business." There. He'd been as polite as he could be with a woman whose type he knew all too well and wanted none of.

Been to that rodeo, didn't want to ride that bull again.

Priscilla pouted and stared at the hard hat. "I'll wait in the car." She spun on her stilettos and stalked across the gravel, wobbling as she went.

Gage breathed in and out through his nostrils before turning to Mr. Langley. "Would you like to see what we're working on?" He fully expected the man to follow his daughter off the site and that would mean kissing goodbye Gage's chance to purchase the downtown property he'd been after for over a year.

Langley's gaze followed his daughter all the way to the limousine. When he turned, he smiled. "Yes.

I'm here to see what you're capable of, and so far, I'm impressed."

Gage led Mr. Langley and Haddie through the site, showed them the drawings and talked about what he was most passionate about, building beautiful buildings that touched the sky.

When Langley departed, Haddie stood beside Gage, her eyes narrowing. "Yup. You have a long way to go on your manners with the ladies, Mr. Tate."

"I can't allow anyone on my site without a hard hat." Period. Gage crossed his arms. "If the hat wasn't a rule, I would have had to ban her from the site because of her open-toed shoes."

Haddie stared at Gage. "What is it about women you don't like, Mr. Tate?"

Everything, he wanted to say, but opted for, "Nothing." Other than they were gold-diggers, looking for the best deal in husband material.

For a long moment, Haddie paused, her gaze raking over him, making him want to squirm like a kid caught smoking in the restroom at school. "Well, Mr. Tate, you have to work with me if you want to shake the image of a cold-hearted son-of-a-bitch the media has labeled you as."

"I'm not cold-hearted," he grumbled, wishing the woman would leave and let him get back to what he did best—making something of nothing.

"The charity ball you'll be throwing will be the place you can change public opinion." Haddie crossed her arms. "But only if you treat women with respect and soften some of those rough edges."

"Why do I even have to go? The goal is to raise money for the charity. The rich and ridiculous will be there spending their money. I don't need to be there."

Haddie poked a finger at his chest. "If you want to sway Mr. Langley to sell you that property, you have to appear, even if you aren't, like a reasonable, caring man. You can't do that by hiding in your penthouse apartment."

He disliked parading in front of a bunch of society men and women who couldn't care less about him but were very interested in the money he could donate to all their causes. Where were the real people? "I hate wearing a damn tux."

"Tough." Haddie poked her finger at his chest again. "You just told a whopping lie to a woman who could convince her daddy that he shouldn't sell his property to you. And unless you want her to call you out on your lie, I suggest you find a suitable date for the charity ball and do it soon." Haddie handed him the hardhat and left.

Gage groaned. Where was he going to find a date for the ball that was only a couple weeks away? He absolutely refused to date a money-hungry socialite. Haddie was right, he did have a problem with women. Especially the kind that strung you along, claiming to love you when all they were interested in was being with the man with the most money. In Gage's book, they were all like that.

His cell phone beeped in his back pocket. He yanked it out and glanced down, groaning again at the text from his friend Tag Bronson.

Billionaires Anonymous Club. Thirty minutes. Be there.

Gage texted, *Too busy.*

Sick? Tag responded.

No

Dying?

Gage sighed and keyed, *No.*

No excuses. We made a promise. Be there!

THIRTY MINUTES LATER...

IF HE'D THOUGHT his morning couldn't get worse, it most certainly could.

"Don't leave love up to luck. Like I told you the first time we met, with the help of my firm and heavily tested computer algorithms, you have a ninety-nine point nine percent chance of finding your perfect match. So, who's next?"

Leslie Lamb, the woman dressed in a soft gray suit, her blond, shoulder-length hair swinging, turned from the video screen to face the group of men seated around the conference table. On the screen was a picture of the first couple to find success through the Billionaire Online Dating System, or BODS as it was shortened to. Frank Cooper Johnson and his BODS match, Emma Jacobs.

Gage tapped his fingertips against the conference table surrounded by members of the Billionaires Anonymous Club, frankly amazed at how the first test of BODS had turned out. Who knew a computer program could pick the perfect match for one of their own? It had to be a lucky coincidence. Computers couldn't account for all the human traits and personality quirks.

But Cooper sat back with the biggest grin on his face, happier than a pig in mud.

So happy, Gage shifted in his seat, an itch crawling across his skin. No man could be that in love. Could he? Didn't he know what would eventually happen? No union lasted these days.

The men had formed the club back when they were five broke college students struggling to get an education at Texas A&M. On their last dime, and facing the distinct possibility of expulsion for various reasons—the most pressing reason having to do with money—they'd made a pact that they'd all become millionaires by the time they turned thirty. They'd formed a plan, stuck with it, finished college, each becoming, not millionaires, but billionaires by age thirty and achieving all their goals.

All except one. The one about getting married

and raising a family. They'd all struggled with that one.

A year ago, Gage thought he'd be the first out the chute for the marriage goal. He'd been dating Lacy Welch, a beautiful blond who claimed to be crazy about him. She'd told him she loved him and he'd believed her. In the back of his mind he had images of the family-life some of his friends had grown up with—kids running around the yard, mothers kissing their babies goodnight. For a brief moment in his ambitious drive to the top, he'd paused, thinking this was his chance. Until he'd proposed to Lacy, asking her to marry him and start a family together.

Boy had he been wrong.

She'd been horrified he'd wanted her to actually bear children. Lacy wanted the marriage without the family, afraid having children would destroy her figure and keep her from traveling the world. If he could promise her no children and an unlimited expense account, she'd marry him.

His ideal shattered, Gage ultimately figured he'd dodged a bullet. He retracted his proposal and went back to work, marriage no longer part of his equation for success.

"Ah, come on guys. It's not that bad." Cooper pulled Emma into his lap. "You heard the lady, I found my perfect match using BODS."

Gage shifted in his seat, ready for this meeting to be over. He had real issues to work through, like finding a date for the charity ball.. "Leslie, you have to change the acronym. BODS might send the wrong signals."

"Sorry, I have too much invested in letterhead, business cards and promo items to change it now." She winked at him.

"Just because it worked for Coop, doesn't mean it'll work for the rest of us." Gage drummed his fingers on the smooth surface of the mahogany conference table. "Sounds to me more like a crap shoot." He leaned back against his seat, ready to tune out of the rest of the conversation.

"You won't know until you give it a try." Taggert Bronson stepped up beside Leslie. "Gage, you have a charity ball coming up in a couple weeks, don't you?"

Gage snapped forward, the ball already making his stomach twist into a knot. He didn't need to bring it to the attention of the rest of his friends. "Yeah, so?"

"Why don't you give the system a shot and take the match it finds you. What's it gonna hurt? At the very least, you'll have a date for the ball."

Gage bristled, hating being the one on the spot for the hair-brained scheme. "Who said I didn't already have a date?"

Tag pinned him with a stare. "Do you?"

Gage thought through all the women he knew for a quick answer, someone he wouldn't mind asking to the ball and solve his problem with having lied to Priscilla. Unfortunately, most of his go-to girls ran in her circle. They might let slip that his invitation had been at the last minute, and if one of them did, his goose would be cooked with Daddy. "Damn it, no."

Sean O'Leary leaned over and nudged his arm. "I'm sure Priscilla Langley or Marilynn Tisdale would love to be your date. You could ask one of them. Maybe both."

"Hell, no." Gage sat up straight, staring across the boardroom table to Leslie. "Do the women you have signing up for this system know they're signing up to be matched with a wealthy man?"

Leslie shook her head. "Not at all. Some of them have money of their own and don't feel a need to marry well. Others may not have the kind of money you gentlemen have, but they are good people with sound ethics and values." She tipped her chin up. "I hand-select all the applicants for my system to ensure honesty and strong moral fiber."

Maxwell Smithson snorted. "Well, that rules us out."

Sean, Tag and Cooper laughed.

Gage didn't, his mind spinning with the possibility of finding a woman he could feel comfortable with to take to that confounded charity ball. "Can I get a woman who's down to earth? I'm sick to death of society debutantes and women who are only interested in the size of a man's bank account."

Leslie held her hand up like she was swearing in at court. "No fortune hunters or debutantes are allowed. Give my system a chance. I promise not all women are after money. Most just want to be treated nicely and maybe find love."

"I'm not looking for love or happily ever after. But I *could* use a date for the ball." He rubbed his chin. A woman unknown to the social elite of Dallas would be good. At least Priscilla wouldn't have any way of knowing he hadn't asked her to the ball until after he'd told Priscilla he had a date. And going through with BODS would get the other guys off his back.

"I'm still not believing you're throwing a ball in the first place," Sean commented. "I thought you hated that kind of event."

Gage grimaced. "Trust me. I'd rather slit my throat. Blame it on my image consultant. She insisted I throw one to demonstrate to the public I have a goddamn heart."

Sean laughed. "You mean it's not obvious to the media that our buddy, Gage Tate, has a heart of gold? What was it the news called you? Heartless, calculating and...what was the other adjective?"

Cooper, Maxwell and Tag answered as one, "Cutthroat."

"Yeah, yeah." Gage glared around the table. "Go ahead and laugh. You're not the one having to show up and smile for the cameras. Most of you are still anonymous." He focused on Leslie again, the notion of finding a date for the ball through BODS no longer completely appalling. "My name has been in the media too much lately. Is it possible to use a different name in your system to find a match?"

Leslie's brows dipped. "That would be dishonest."

"He's right." Tag tapped his chin. "Gage Tate would be an immediate giveaway."

Sean leaned toward the table. "Why not use your first name?"

"Austin?" Gage considered.

"Sure." Tag grinned. "No one associates Austin Tate with Gage Tate, Texas's most eligible bachelor. And it wouldn't be dishonest since it *is* your name."

Gage lifted the monogrammed pen in front of him and flipped it between his fingers, thinking. Haddie had been pushing him to ask one of the daughters of the charity matrons as a sign of good will. If he had a date already lined up for the event, he'd be off the hook. He wouldn't be pressured into escorting a society princess to an event he already dreaded as much as going to the dentist. "Okay." He inhaled and let it out slowly. "I'll do it. But I want to test her out first."

Max chuckled. "You're not taking a car for a test drive."

"In a way, I am." Gage didn't do anything without doing his homework first. He wouldn't be where he was today if he left things to chance. Not since Lacy, anyway. He refused to be humiliated like that, ever again. "I want to know that she's genuine and down to earth, but not so much of a redneck that she can't perform in public."

Emma's eyes narrowed. "I get it. You want a kind of Cinderella test."

Gage stared at Emma. "What?"

"You know." Emma leaned forward. "You want someone who is comfortable dusting furniture or mowing her own lawn, but who can also pull off wearing a dress and smiling in public. You don't want someone who will embarrass you."

"Yeah, I guess," Gage frowned, figuring Emma must think he was a complete jerk. "Hey, we're talking about a ball, not the rest of my damn life. Whomever I take can't be intimidated by the high-rollers who'll be there. I wouldn't want her feeling uncomfortable."

Emma nodded. "Of course. Still you don't want a woman who lets the pretty dress and fancy car go to her head."

"Yeah. I've had my fill of Priscilla Tisdales and Marilyn Langleys." He mentally added Lacy Welch to that list.

"You got them backwards. That's Priscilla Langley and Marilyn Tisdale," Sean corrected. "Although, either one of those women know what to wear and say in front of the big shots of Dallas."

Coop snorted. "They ought to, they've been groomed since birth to marry rich."

Gage shuddered at the thought of taking Priscilla

or Marilyn to anything. "Can't stand either of those women. Plastic all the way through. Do they still make women who aren't only interested in money?"

Emma snorted. "We're not all money-hungry."

Gage turned to Leslie. "Seriously, do you have one of those?"

"I don't like the way this conversation is going." Emma Jacobs climbed out of Frank's lap and shook her head. "Whoever the system pulls out of the hat, you need to remember she's a real, live person with feelings. Frankly, all this talk is lacking in class and humility."

"Right," Leslie added. "This is a matchmaking application, but the people on both ends of the match are just that—people with emotions and feelings. I won't have anyone mistreated. Do you understand?"

"I do." Gage stood. "But also understand, that I'm a busy man with little time to waste on a dead end. If the woman doesn't work out, there's not second date and I'll have to find someone else to go with to the ball."

Leslie's lips pressed together. "Maybe you're not ready for my online dating system."

Gage's cheeks burned. He knew he was being a jerk but, damn it, he didn't want to go to the ball in the first place. In the second place, he really didn't have time to find a date. Having Leslie call him out on his rude behavior didn't sit well with him either.

"Look, I've agreed to do it. When do we start?"

Once he'd set his mind on something, Gage rarely turned back.

"Don't worry." Tag patted Leslie's arm. "He's all bark, no bite."

"Yeah," Cooper said. "We'll make sure he does right by whomever he's matched with."

"Guys, I'm in the room," Gage bit out. "Let's do this before I change my mind."

"Right. You only have two weeks before the big to do." Max said.

Sean grinned. "You'll need time to find and test drive your new ride."

"You did *not* just say that." Emma shook her head and gave Gage a pointed look. "Don't hurt the girl."

Gage raised his hand. "I swear, I'll do my best not to. If all fails, I'll let her down easy." Which was more than he could say for how Lacy had smashed his idiotic dreams.

Leslie hesitated a moment longer, her gaze studying him for the longest.

Gage didn't know he'd been holding his breath until she gave a nod.

Her gaze remained narrowed. "Okay then, step into my office and I'll have you fill out the online profile and preferences."

"So, *you're* the next guinea pig." Cooper rose and clapped a hand to Gage's back. "As someone said to me not long ago, *You won't regret it.*"

For a man known to be as cool as granite and just

as hard to break, Gage's stomach churned and his palms sweat as he sat at Leslie's computer, entering his life story and the laundry list of requirements for his dream girl. As with all his undertakings, he was thorough.

He closed his eyes as he pushed ENTER, praying this wouldn't end up being a really bad mistake.

ABOUT THE AUTHOR

ELLE JAMES also writing as MYLA JACKSON is a *New York Times* and *USA Today* Bestselling author of books including cowboys, intrigues and paranormal adventures that keep her readers on the edges of their seats. With over eighty works in a variety of sub-genres and lengths she has published with Harlequin, Samhain, Ellora's Cave, Kensington, Cleis Press, and Avon. When she's not at her computer, she's traveling, snow skiing, boating, or riding her ATV, dreaming up new stories. Learn more about Elle James at www.ellejames.com

Website | Facebook | Twitter | GoodReads |
Newsletter | BookBub | Amazon

Or visit her alter ego Myla Jackson at
mylajackson.com
Website | Facebook | Twitter | Newsletter

Follow Me!
www.ellejames.com
ellejames@ellejames.com

ALSO BY ELLE JAMES

Hellfire Series

Declan's Defenders

Full Force (#3)

Driving Force (#4)

Tactical Force (#5)

Disruptive Force (#6)

Mission: Six

One Intrepid SEAL

Two Dauntless Hearts

Three Courageous Words

Four Relentless Days

Five Ways to Surrender

Six Minutes to Midnight

Hearts & Heroes Series

Wyatt's War (#1)

Mack's Witness (#2)

Ronin's Return (#3)

Sam's Surrender (#4)

Take No Prisoners Series

SEAL's Honor (#1)

SEAL'S Desire (#2)

SEAL's Embrace (#3)

SEAL's Obsession (#4)

SEAL's Proposal (#5)

Navy SEAL Captive

Navy SEAL To Die For

Navy SEAL Six Pack

Devil's Shroud Series

Deadly Reckoning (#1)

Deadly Engagement (#2)

Deadly Liaisons (#3)

Deadly Allure (#4)

Deadly Obsession (#5)

Deadly Fall (#6)

Covert Cowboys Inc Series

Triggered (#1)

Taking Aim (#2)

Bodyguard Under Fire (#3)

Cowboy Resurrected (#4)

Navy SEAL Justice (#5)

Navy SEAL Newlywed (#6)

High Country Hideout (#7)

Clandestine Christmas (#8)

Thunder Horse Series

Hostage to Thunder Horse (#1)

Thunder Horse Heritage (#2)

Thunder Horse Redemption (#3)

Christmas at Thunder Horse Ranch (#4)

Demon Series

Hot Demon Nights (#1)

Demon's Embrace (#2)

Tempting the Demon (#3)

Lords of the Underworld

Witch's Initiation (#1)

Witch's Seduction (#2)

The Witch's Desire (#3)

Possessing the Witch (#4)

Stealth Operations Specialists (SOS)

Nick of Time

Alaskan Fantasy

Blown Away

Stranded

Feel the Heat

The Heart of a Cowboy

Protecting His Heroine

Warrior's Conquest

Rogues

Enslaved by the Viking Short Story

Conquests

Smokin' Hot Firemen

Love on the Rocks

Protecting the Colton Bride

Protecting the Colton Bride & Colton's Cowboy Code

Heir to Murder

Secret Service Rescue

High Octane Heroes

Haunted

Engaged with the Boss

Cowboy Brigade

Time Raiders: The Whisper

Bundle of Trouble

Killer Body

Operation XOXO

An Unexpected Clue

Baby Bling

Under Suspicion, With Child

Texas-Size Secrets

Cowboy Sanctuary

Lakota Baby

Dakota Meltdown

Beneath the Texas Moon

Made in the USA
Las Vegas, NV
04 July 2024

91799621R00115